free radical

free radical

*

Claire Rudolf Murphy

CLARION BOOKS * NEW YORK

Clarion Books
a Houghton Mifflin Company imprint
215 Park Avenue South, New York, NY 10003
Copyright © 2002 by Claire Rudolf Murphy

The text was set in 12-point Adobe Garamond.

www.houghtonmifflinbooks.com

Printed in the U.S.A.

Library of Congress Cataloging-in-Publication Data

Murphy, Claire Rudolf.
Free radical / by Claire Rudolf Murphy.
p. cm.
Summary: In Fairbanks, Alaska, in the middle of the summer Little
League baseball season, fifteen-year-old Luke is stunned when his
mother confesses that she is wanted by the FBI for her role in the death
of a student during an anti-Vietnam War protest thirty years ago.
ISBN 0-618-11134-4
[1. Fugitives from justice—Fiction. 2. Baseball—Fiction.
3. Fairbanks (Alaska)—Fiction.] I. Title.

PZ7.M9525 Fr 2002
[Fic]—dc21   2001042268

HAD 10 9 8 7 6 5 4 3 2 1

With affection and appreciation to the SCBWI
Fairbanks group for years of friendship and support

Acknowledgments

Many people helped in the writing and research for this book. I wish to thank Briana Staege for talking to me about her life in a wheelchair; Harvey West and Roland La March of Golden West for their help in understanding modified vans and wheelchairs; public information officers Lieutenant Barren Bobell and Lieutenant George VeVea of the Northern California Women's Facility; Greg Schoonard of Valley State Prison for Women; Sergeant Jim Knudson of the Alameda County Sheriff's office; Chuck Canterbury of Fort Richardson, Anchorage, Alaska; Annie Jennings of American Legion Post 11 in Fairbanks; and Douglas Jones from the Veterans of Foreign Wars office in Spokane.

Also attorneys Dan Callahan, Paul Canarsky, Ken Cavell, Carroll Gray, Mark Hanley, Dick Madsen, and Kermit Rudolf for endless help on legal matters; my son, Conor, and his baseball teammates over the years, who along with my husband, Bob Murphy, have taught me about baseball; the writers to whom the book is dedicated: Nancy White Carlstrom, Julie Coghill, Arnold Griese, Mike Mertes, Debbie Miller, Sue Quinlan, Marilyn Richardson, Linda Russell, Randy Stowell, Susan Thierman, Deb Vanasse, Marie Ward, and Ellen Wood, along with Mary Cronk Farrell and Meghan Nuttall Sayres. Thanks also for the support of my editor, Virginia Buckley, and my agent, Liza Voges, who have continued to believe in this story, and my husband for information about restorative justice and his loving support, and for the support of my daughter, Megan.

Chapter 1

When I was six years old, I figured out there wasn't a Santa Claus. Pretty young, huh? This kid Ted Callahan was talking about how stupid it was to believe in Santa Claus. But my neighbor Curt Perry said it was smart, because you could get more Christmas presents that way.

At dinner that night I said to my mom, "There isn't a Santa Claus. How come you pretended there was?"

"Oh, honey." That's what she said—"Oh, honey." Right then I should have learned that you can't believe in things straight out. But no. It took me eight more years.

Maybe that's because all I thought about was sports, especially baseball. I'd played it every summer since I was six years old—the same year I learned about Santa Claus.

In summer Alaskans go wild. Hunting, fishing, boating— you name it. For me, summer spells baseball. Our season may be short, but in Fairbanks, where I live, you can play baseball all night long because the midnight sun hardly ever sets.

I'd played Little League ever since I was a little kid, when I started out hitting that stupid ball off the stupid stand in T-ball. I'd moved up through the ranks in Minors, Majors, and now I was in my second and last year in Juniors. But in all that time I'd never made a postseason All Star team. This was going to be my year. And it was—until Mom's thirty-one-year-old secret blasted across the headlines.

Alaska is the perfect place to hide—far away from the lower Forty-eight and full of people who don't care where you came from as long as you can handle the weather.

Mom's changed her name back, but I can't. I've been Luke McHenry for fifteen years.

I think I first started wondering the day of the bomb scare at my middle school. But as I look back, there were signs all along the way. I just didn't read them.

The day before school let out, kids were wired, and the teachers had long since given up on getting any work done, except Ms. Simmons in algebra. She had us graphing fractions until the last bell rang.

Anyway, right in the middle of social studies, the fire alarm went off. Kids actually started applauding, until Mr. Taylor glared at them. "It could be a real fire."

I grabbed my yearbook, the one with me making the game-winning basket against Denali Middle School, and started out the door. In the hallway the assistant principal waved us away from the exit we usually used and down another hallway. Once we were outside, the teachers directed all the students onto the playing fields, far away from the building. The whole school stood jammed together. But people were strangely quiet. This was not your ordinary fire drill. The principal, Mr. Shepherd, stood on a wooden box and started speaking through a bullhorn. Unlike a school assembly, he didn't need to wait for silence.

"Students and teachers, I need your complete and undivided attention. An object, which police suspect could be a bomb, has been found in the girls' restroom. Right now the police department's SWAT team is removing it from the building." At that, everybody started talking and it took a while for the kids to quiet down again.

"No one will be allowed back in the building until it has been completely checked out. You are to leave immediately for home by bus or on foot." Just then a fleet of buses pulled into the parking lot. "Unfortunately we regret that tonight's eighth-grade graduation dance has had to be canceled. Please listen to the news for information about school tomorrow. Thank you, students, for your cooperation." By now some of the girls were crying.

We used to joke about stuff like that, but not since all the real school shootings. I was glad to go home. I didn't care about the dance. Everybody just stands around until a slow song comes on about once an hour.

Talk about a bomb. That first game was a disaster, with us losing, 15–5. Back on the Padres I wouldn't have a prayer of making All Stars if we weren't any better than last year. It didn't look promising. Hardly anybody could hit. Dan's pitching was way off. I played catcher and nobody could handle my throws.

Our new coach started Scott Lemming at shortstop, after having preached for two weeks in practice about the importance of good sportsmanship. Lemming mouthed off, in finer form than last season, calling Bud Sampson, a new player, "Doughboy," among other endearments. Lemming is the original Pillsbury Doughboy and the slowest base runner on our team.

Sid, my mom's new husband, would have gotten me switched off the Padres if he'd known Lemming was still on the team. I'd been stuck on a Majors team with him for two years and now Juniors for two more. Last year, in front of all the parents at the team party, Lemming said, "I wouldn't play with the Padres again for a million bucks." But here he was again, no richer.

Sid was out doing electrical work in some Eskimo village, and Mom never complained about things like that. So lucky me got to have Lemming as a teammate once more.

Sid wasn't what you would call macho. In fact, I was already bigger than him. He was short and skinny and didn't have a deep voice or much hair on his chest. Nothing great in the athletic department, either. But there was just something about him that people didn't mess with.

In the fourth inning when I missed a throw to tag out the runner, I tore off my catcher's mask and swore. Sid would have told the coach to bench me. Mom sat watching from inside her 1981 Honda Civic and wouldn't have heard it. How she could stay locked in there, on a warm, cloudless night, I never understood. But that's how she usually watched my games, unless Sid was with her.

At one point Lemming slapped me on the back in the dugout. "What'sa matter, Big Mac—your daddy never play catch with ya?" I felt like punching him in the mouth. Didn't he know that my dad had been killed years ago?

Some drunk driver had broadsided him and he was killed instantly. He died before he even knew that Mom was pregnant with me. When I was in fourth grade and had to write my autobiography, I got real upset when I learned the whole story. "I hate people who drink. They should all be thrown in jail," I remember yelling.

Mom had leaned over and held me for a while. "I'm sorry he's gone, Luke." I couldn't say I missed my dad because I'd never had him around. It's just that I would have liked to know something about him. Lately I've been worrying how tall I was going to get. At five foot six, I could use more inches. I couldn't help wondering how tall my father had been, if he'd been athletic, if he'd been a good sport.

Mom had one old photo of him fishing but it was mostly river and sky. I couldn't tell much about what he looked like. I didn't know anything about Mom's relatives, either. She said they said Alaska was too far away to visit. Mom said she hated all the busyness of life Outside, so she never wanted to leave. That's what she told me.

Mom is five foot five, but that wasn't much help because I don't look at all like her. She's kind of overweight, is not athletic, and had really short blond hair then. I'm wiry and coordinated, and a natural athlete, even if my coaches don't always recognize it. I've got this brown—almost black—hair. I have blue eyes, she has green. Girls say mine sparkle. You can't really say that about Mom's.

After the game I was furious about the loss, but Dan just shrugged it off. All he seemed to care about was going fishing with his grandpa from Seattle. We didn't hang out as much in the summer because he had relatives visiting all the time.

So when Lemming invited me to go paintballing, I jumped at the chance. It didn't make Lemming any less of a jerk, but I'd been dying to go ever since Dan let me try out the new paintball gun he'd gotten for his birthday. The power had about blown me away.

I had to think fast about what to tell Mom, because she would never agree to paintball. When I was younger, my friends and I would go around shooting up bad guys. *Baaaw . . . baaam . . . booom . . .* complete with sound effects.

Mom would go nuts and actually start screaming. "Stop it! Stop it right now. No guns in this house." My friends looked at her like she was crazy, especially since she was usually super calm compared to their mothers.

I never had one gun during my childhood, not even a squirt gun, except for the one my neighbor Curt gave me out of pity. He had about a dozen, of course, and his dad even took him duck hunting every September. I used to hope they would take me along when I was older, but they moved when I was ten. I always wondered if my dad had liked to hunt.

I hid Curt's old G.I. Joe machine gun under my bed and pretended everything else was one—Legos, pieces of wood, even bananas. You can't keep kids away from what they really want. You'd think adults would learn that.

Mom would talk to me and my friends later, when she had calmed down. "Boys, it could be real people dying. No matter how exciting war seems, it all comes down to death."

"We're just playing," we'd always say. But she didn't understand.

She did understand about some things, though. When other kids were getting in trouble for lousy grades, she would just say, "You don't have to be perfect. But use the talents God gave you."

Paintball: the perfect way to forget a disastrous game. As I tried to settle down and come up with a story, Mom waved me over.

"Luke, I don't want you going back into that school tomorrow," she said, leaning out the car window.

School. I'd forgotten all about it. As far as I was concerned, summer had already started.

Chapter 2

"You want to go over to Scott Lemming's house?" She sounded surprised.

"No, paintball," I wanted to shout. But I couldn't tell her that. So instead I said, "Mom, we had a lousy game, but it's a new season. People can change, and the only way we can work together is if we get to know each other." She stared at me as if I were some alien being. "Besides, Dan's going fishing with his grandpa." Mention of Dan's relatives always seemed to get to her.

"Well, all right. Be good, Luke." She always said that. "I can't believe you'll be starting high school in September." Lemming kept beeping the horn on his brother Jason's truck.

"Now, don't call later, begging to stay overnight. I don't even know his parents." No problem there. I wouldn't have been caught dead staying at Lemming's house.

"His brother said he'd bring me back home around eleven."

"I love you, Luke."

"I love you, too, Mom," I mumbled.

I was stuck in the back of Rick's extended-cab truck with Bud Sampson, who wouldn't stop yakking. "Man, I've been playing paintball for years down in Tacoma. Fairbanks is so behind the times. I just about had a hernia when I found out the Army had transferred my dad to this icebox." I stared out the window, amazed that somebody could be a bigger pain than Lemming.

When we were almost there, Rick said, "Now, be conservative, guys. Don't run through all your balls right away. They are spendy." I wasn't sure what he meant by conservative.

"That's right," Bud said. "I've seen guys blow through a hundred dollars' worth of paintballs in one night."

The referee divided us into two teams of twelve each. Except for us four teenagers, the rest were military guys, a few Army, mostly Air Force. Lemming and his brother got put on the Green team, Bud and me on the Blue team. Some teammate Bud would make. Besides his mouth he carried an extra thirty pounds, easy. But at least I figured he'd know how to shoot. What a joke. Why do people have to lie all the time?

I hadn't lied to my mom that night. I just hadn't told her the truth.

The Green team looked meaner, but we had some big guys—the kind you wouldn't want to mess with.

After shooting practice, which I stunk at, the referee walked us out to the enclosed, netted course. It was about a quarter mile wide and deep with a long uphill, complete with bunkers and trees for cover.

"Keep your protective masks on at all times, and stop when the whistle blows or you're outta here," the ref warned.

First we played Capture the Flag. It sounds like something you'd play on the school playground, but it was far from that. My team lined up at the Blue flag and the Green team on their side.

Thurrrrrrr! went the whistle, my heart exploding. We all ran and ducked behind bunkers. Then nothing happened. *Nada.* Just total and complete silence. Finally this crazy guy from our team yelled out, "Screw this. I'm tired of sitting around."

Off he went, sprinting through the center area, enemy guns firing at him. *Pshlat, pshlat, pshlat.* Down he went. I stayed crouched behind my bunker, paralyzed, unable to lift my arm to shoot. All I could do was watch orange paintballs fly over my head, splat off the tires, nail a victim. Were combat soldiers as cowardly as me? I wondered.

After that wild charge, things slowed down a bit. Bud nudged me. I hadn't realized he'd been positioned all along right behind me in the same bunker. He didn't know what to do any more than I did.

We started creeping forward, tentatively shooting our guns but hitting nothing. Two Green guys approached from the bunker above us. Bud and I looked at each other, then started firing. *Pow! Pow!* Splatter City and they were down.

One of them called out, "Paint check." What a wimp. Of course we'd gotten him. He had paint all over his stomach. The ref stopped the action. "Hold your positions. Put your barrel plugs in."

I stuck the plastic stick down the barrel and took my first breath since the game had begun. Looking around, I finally had a chance to study the course. The bunkers were actually piles of tires covered by camouflage netting. At first they had looked like real rocks. The two guys we had nailed, determined goners by the ref, headed down the hill to the "dead" area, which was full of players who had already been shot and been eliminated from the game.

Finally, the ref yelled, "Barrel plugs out, goggles on!" then blew the whistle. I started firing and immediately hit somebody right below me. A Green guy yelled out, "Shit," and fell, dumping all his paintballs out. He put his plug in and knelt down to pick them up. "What the—" It was Scott, alias Lemming the Younger. I couldn't help smiling.

With three of our men left standing, Bud got to capture the Green flag and we Blues won the game. Of course the Army guys were good, but it turned out that the Air Force guys weren't any better shots than us teens.

One of the friendly ones walked out with me. "Going hunting like you do, you Alaskan kids probably shoot guns more than we do. We just fly planes." He looked a lot older, maybe thirty, but in great shape, especially his muscled biceps. I thought about starting a weightlifting program. Couldn't hurt.

When I entered the "dead" area, Scott was bragging about how many guys he'd taken down. "But somebody shot me in the arm when my goggles fogged up, and that's how I ended up down here."

"It was me, Lemming, and you lost all your balls." Everybody started laughing, especially Bud.

Lemming glared at me. "Just you wait, McHenry."

He never did get me. One Army guy wore an ammo belt and went through 700 paintballs in two hours, at $7.50 per hundred. I stretched out $15 worth over four hours. Lemming and his brother kept buying more balls, but I didn't have that kind of money. So Bud and I started picking up unexploded ones that had fallen on the ground.

"I wouldn't do that," the ref warned us. "Those balls are all swollen up from rainwater and could blow up inside your gun."

But they didn't. Nor did the paint grenade I cradled in my hands all the way home. I'd uncovered it during the final maneuver, when I crawled around in the dirt with Bud. Lemming wanted it. But it was mine, all mine.

When Rick pulled up in the driveway, I glanced up at our living-room window. Mom had her face plastered to the glass. It looked distorted, like when you stand in front of one of those funny mirrors at the amusement park—the ones where you can gain or lose fifty pounds with one step either direction.

She met me at the front door, her blond hair spiked with sweat, her green eyes glazed over like a TV screen with no picture.

"Luke, why didn't you tell me where you were going?"

"What do you mean?"

"That you went to play paint whatever, instead of going to Scott's house."

"Scott's brother suggested it later, and I didn't think you'd care as long as I was home on time." I put my arm around her. "Besides, it offers great hand-eye coordination practice, Mom. I needed some help after tonight's game."

"Don't sweet-talk me, buster," she said, her voice rising a notch. "You should have called me."

She grabbed my arm and dug her nails in, leading me up the stairs into the living room.

"Ouch. That hurts."

"Well, it's going to hurt a lot more if you lose my trust. You want to make your own decisions? Then make sure you don't hide things from me."

"Okay, Mom. I'm sorry." That usually calmed her down. Maybe because I so seldom said it. I reached out to give her a hug and noticed the television was on. A reporter was standing in front of my school. "The Fairbanks Police De- partment's SWAT team was called to Chena Middle School to investigate a bomb threat today. The bomb left in the girls' restroom turned out to be a fake and deemed not dangerous. Police continued to comb the entire building. The school has now been declared completely safe and students are encouraged to attend tomorrow, the last day of school. School officials commended the students for their cooperation and maturity this morning and all the parents for their concern."

Mom stood transfixed. "You're not going back there, Luke. You can never be too careful about something like this."

I started laughing. "Fine with me. But it's probably just some stupid punk who doesn't want to go to school anymore."

"If that was a real bomb, people could have been killed."

The story continued after the commercial. "Many local officials think bomb scares like this could lead to more serious acts of school violence," the newscaster said. Mom looked over at me, nodding her head.

A clip of a school shooting appeared on the screen. Students were shown running out of a building. The scene of two teenage boys appearing in court followed.

Mom turned off the television.

"Killers like that should be nailed to the wall, no matter how old they are," I said.

"Do you think that solves anything?" Mom asked, walking down the hallway. "Let's help out at the soup kitchen this weekend, Luke. Focus on something positive."

"The one in the basement of that Catholic church?" She nodded. "You getting religion, Mom?"

"Like you said, things change." She hugged me hard. I still held the paint grenade in my right hand, and all I could think about was not pressing it against her shoulder.

"I'll bet those parents would give anything right now to get their children back," Mom said, not letting go.

Chapter

On Memorial Day I woke up to a dead house. Not a sound but chirping birds and a couple of power mowers along the block. I sat up, remembering the paint grenade I'd hidden under my bed. I grabbed it and paced around the room, clutching it to my chest. *Poogh. Boom.* Then I dropped to the floor, pretending the grenade had exploded against my stomach. I lay there for a long time, wondering what it would be like to die.

Maybe my dad had been a military man, cool and calm like the paintball ref or wild like one of the Army guys, blowing through thousands of balls. I didn't know much about him. After a while I buried the grenade in my underwear drawer and went to eat breakfast.

I didn't see how Mom could still be sleeping with the sun beating through the windows. Outside, the lawn sprouted with dandelions and mushrooms from the recent rainfall. I'd promised Sid to mow the lawn once a week. But he wasn't going to be home for a while. Mom didn't really care if it ever got mowed.

Things get out of control fast during an Alaskan summer. Because the sun's up almost twenty-four hours a day, the grass grows like a weightlifter on steroids. And if there's been any rain, the place gets blanketed with mushrooms, especially the puffball kind. I used to mow them over, too lazy to pull them out. Didn't realize that they were poisonous, and by making them explode, I was spreading their seeds in astronomical numbers. Pretty stupid, as Mom would say.

That reminds me of the story about the mushroom who walks into a bar. He sits down and the bartender says, "You can't sit here."

"Why not?" asks the mushroom.

"We don't serve your kind," says the bartender.

"But I'm a fun guy," answers the mushroom.

Fungi. I didn't get the joke the first time Dan told it to me. Just like I didn't get a lot of stuff.

Around noon I took off on my bike, hoping to find some kids at the park to play catch with. Dead. So I kept biking and ended up in the hills, at the cemetery on Birch Hill. A bunch of military guys and some other people were holding a ceremony for Memorial Day.

The color guard lifted their guns and sounded a twenty-one-gun salute. Then a young soldier, who looked like he could still be in high school, played taps on his bugle. I got the creeps when three old guys, wearing these ridiculous purple pointed hats, started reading lists of dead Alaskan soldiers. I wanted to leave but couldn't seem to move. So I stood there, remembering how during paintball I'd gotten off on shooting people. Do guys in war love it, too, or is it different killing people for real?

Four fighter jets flew overhead in formation. One dropped away, and three planes took off into the distance. The air filled with eerie silence. Afterward people moved from gravesite to gravesite, placing wreaths and bowing their heads in prayer.

Later, when they all were driving away, one geezer in an old Chevy sedan pulled over and rolled down his window. "Glad to see you here, young man. Pretty soon us old veterans won't be around to remember these brave soldiers."

"You know the maneuver the planes did overhead?" The old man nodded. "What is that called?"

"Glad you asked. It's called the missing-man formation. It honors the soldiers who died in combat. I hope you got a chance to see the replica of the Vietnam Wall down at Bicentennial Park. Today's the last day, you know."

My social studies teacher, Mr. Taylor, had promised extra credit if we went, but I'd forgotten.

I wished I'd met the old man before Taylor's big U.S. history project. We had to talk to a veteran from any war. Most of the kids could talk to their grandfathers about World War II or the Korean War. "Too bad I don't have a grandfather to call," I said at the kitchen table the night before the assignment was due.

"Go talk to Charlie next door. He fought in Vietnam."

Charlie, the one with more dandelions in his yard than we had. I took a zero instead.

You'd think I'd have better things to do than hang around a cemetery. But I started walking around, studying the gravestones. I did the math and figured out that some of these guys had died when they were only nineteen or twenty.

When I got home Mom was on the deck talking to Sid. She handed the phone over to me and Sid asked about my first game.

"It was okay." I paused. "Actually, it was lousy. Our team sucks again. Sid, I'll never have a shot at All Stars stuck with these losers."

"Listen, Luke," Sid said in his quiet voice. "It's a chance to work on all aspects of your game and help the team."

Right, I thought, just like Lemming. "You'd think I could have a decent team for once. Maybe I'll just quit."

"You won't make All Stars by quitting. Just make your throws so sweet, so solid, that they can't miss 'em. The rest will take care of itself." He cleared his throat. "I hope to see that new and improved attitude when I come home next weekend."

I'd been wanting to ask Mom some questions about my dad. But today she seemed sad. I guess Memorial Day was a day to think about the dead. It was so beautiful out, I figured it might help her mood if she went someplace.

"Great day for a bike ride," I suggested. Weird. Now I was

talking like her. She used to be the one to make me get off the computer or television and go outside.

When she didn't answer me, I stared down at her garden. All I could see were old piles of leaves. Where were her flowers? I ran down the deck stairs, grabbed a rake, and attacked the brown moldy mounds. Underneath, small green shoots were sprouting up through the dirt even though they'd had no water or sunshine.

"Mom, look," I yelled. "These suckers are still kicking." But she wasn't on the deck anymore.

Usually her plants come back year after year, no matter what. But one year most of her plants died because there hadn't been enough snow to insulate them over the winter. That spring she had to buy new ones and start all over.

I was raking so hard, I didn't notice her waiting by the shed alongside her dusty bike. She looked different, younger. "I thought you wanted to go riding," she said.

We stopped at a gas station to fill up her tires. When she didn't ask where we were going, I headed downtown. On the bike trail along the Chena River this guy with long bushy hair and a beard stepped right in our path. He carried a sign—JESUS SAVES—and looked like he hadn't taken a shower in months.

Staring right at Mom, he said, "You can't protect your family. All you can do is put yourself in the hands of Jesus."

Mom started talking to him even though she always brushed off the missionaries knocking on our door. Finally, I told her I was leaving, or she would have stayed all day.

We rode by Bicentennial Park, where a crowd milled around the replica of the wall. People were pointing to names, taping on notes and letters, leaving flowers. Up in the gazebo a woman about Mom's age started reading a list of names, pausing after each one.

"I've got to get out of here," Mom said, taking off on her bike.

When I finally caught up with her, tears were running down her face. "Is somebody's name on the wall that you know? We could try to find it. There's supposed to be a directory to help you locate people."

She shook her head and kept on riding. It couldn't be my dad she was upset about. He'd died long after the Vietnam War.

Chapter 4

One night I had an unbelievable game—three hits, four RBI's, no errors at catcher. About time. If I didn't show them I could do it in the regular league, I'd never have a chance for All Stars or high school ball.

Too bad Sid wasn't there to see it. Of course, he always liked to say, "It's easy to be a good sport when you're winning."

On the way home Mom asked me, "What's your favorite part of baseball?"

I thought for a minute. "Running the bases. Probably because I'm not a home-run hitter like Barry Bonds," I said, shrugging my shoulders. "But when I do get a hit or even a walk, then I'm in control and can just go for it. Batting—you're under the gun. You hit it or you die. Fielding—you catch it or you die. But running," I said, "then I feel free."

"But you can get caught stealing a base," Mom said.

"Not if you're smart."

It had been an early game, and afterward I turned on the television, just as a news show started. They were doing a piece on Dusty Baker, the manager of the San Francisco Giants, my team, top of the National League West. Mom sat down to join me so she could tell Sid about it. Sid loves the Giants as much as I do.

But you know how those shows are. They hook you with a teaser of their best story and then don't show it until the end of the hour. The program started off with a piece about something called victim-offender mediation. This kid had robbed somebody's home, and later, after he got caught and confessed, the family met with him and told him how angry they were. They asked him questions, too, like why had he done it. It was actually pretty interesting, but when the commercial came on, I noticed that Mom had left the room.

The people actually forgave the kid if he promised not to do it again. They showed a woman who had killed this lady while driving drunk. Five years later she met with the lady's husband and parents to apologize. I didn't understand how they could face each other like that without breaking down.

I thought that story would have held Mom's interest. She did return for the Dusty Baker segment. Not only is he a baseball genius, he speaks Spanish and visits schools all over the Bay area.

A few days later Mom called from her store, the Quilting Bee, and asked me to get some Chinese takeout for lunch.

The Quilting Bee is this funky little fabric place. No chain store would do for Mom and her best friend, Kathleen. Now that I think about it, I wonder where they got the money to start it. Some inheritance of Kathleen's, probably. I guess her family is rich. Mom sure didn't have any money.

I used to hang out there all the time, playing in the stockroom, shaking all the little bottles of craft paint, even running up and down the aisles when the store was empty. When I got older, Dan and I would stop by and hit up Mom or Kathleen for money for ice cream or fries.

Crafty types like the store because it has fabric, beads, and buttons that you can't get anyplace else in town. It's located right in downtown Fairbanks, stuck between two stores that sell handmade Eskimo yo-yo's and little bottles of gold dust to the tourists.

When I stopped by the store with the food, I found Kathleen in the back office. "None for me, Lukey—I'm too wired to eat."

"No more Lukey, Kathleen. I'm not a kid anymore." She twirled around and kissed me on the cheek. I knew she'd keep calling me whatever she wanted.

I didn't dare call her Kathy. Nobody did. Maybe that's why she and Mom worked so well as partners—they were opposites. Mom did the creative stuff like choosing fabrics and arranging the store; Kathleen did the tough stuff like hiring and firing and cussing out sales reps.

Kathleen always had some new guy on the line, too.

Mom had never even looked at a man until Sid came around last year to work on the electrical system at the store.

"Oh, Amy," Kathleen called through the swinging door. "Come meet Luke." I wanted to duck out but was trapped. "Amy. In here, darling."

I watched a wheelchair motor smoothly through the door. Too embarrassed to look at the girl, I looked at her chair. The wheelchair had a name on it—Jazzy. And it was—with a tan leather seat, blue metallic base, and two sets of wheels—medium in the back, and mini ones in the front where the foot holders were. I had never realized a wheelchair could look so good.

"So how was your canoe trip?"

Canoe trip?

A low, husky voice answered, and I finally looked at the girl. "The weather couldn't have been better. Did you have a nice weekend?"

Kathleen beamed at the question.

Amy was pretty, even in a wheelchair. "We want to meet him. Don't we, Luke?"

Who was this girl? She had long blond hair that hung kind of wavy, below her shoulders, and big brown eyes. Why did she know all about Kathleen's love life?

"I guess I don't have to introduce you two. Well, back to work." Kathleen waved me away and returned to her desk.

I had no choice but to follow Amy as she rolled her way back out to the front of the store. I vaguely remembered a girl in a wheelchair weaving through the halls at school last year. But I had never actually looked at her. Was this the same person? If so, how could I have missed her gorgeous face?

Mom motioned me over to the register and handed me a twenty-dollar bill. Amy had started adding spools of thread to a display stand, the supply box positioned nearby on a stool. I watched her, amazed at how much she could do with her buff upper body.

I couldn't resist walking over. "You look familiar. Did you go to Chena?"

She nodded but kept on working, as if the wheelchair wasn't even there. In a way, it just looked like a jazzed-up computer chair.

"But only for a couple of months, after my dad got transferred up here a year ago with the Army. I've just finished up my freshman year at McKinley." Amy finally looked up at me. "How about you?"

"I just finished eighth grade at Chena. But I'll be at McKinley in the fall." What an idiot. I had to announce how young I was.

It didn't seem to bother her. "Well, a word to the wise. Avoid Dermot for English and definitely don't take bio with Martinez. You'll like the rotating schedule." She stopped when Mom finished up with a customer. "You'd better go. I don't want to get fired my first week on the job."

I turned and headed to the door, not reacting when she

called out, "See you later, Luke." It's not like she had guys, I thought, stuck in a wheelchair. So why was she toying with me?

Mom was busy with a customer when I got back, so I returned to the backroom, where I found Kathleen sitting on the couch, feet up, eyes closed.

"Catching a beauty nap?" I said, laughing.

"Mellow out, boy. I'm doing TM—transcendental meditation. It helps me connect with my deepest levels of consciousness." Kathleen opened her eyes. "I should sign you up for a class sometimes. I'll bet it would help you focus better in baseball."

"Maybe. If it could help me win a spot on the All Star team—"

"I wish I could interest your mother in TM. With all the stress and pollutants in this world, we need to do everything we can to rid our bodies of free radicals."

"Free radicals?"

"Yeah. The bad guys that run around in our bodies causing cancer and loads of other problems." Kathleen dug out a bottle of vitamins from her purse and started reading. "'Free radicals are cell-destroying oxidizers that, like rust on metal, begin to eat away and break through the cell membrane, causing serious damage to the cells.'" She looked up at me. "Free radicals are out there, just trying to drag us down." She started pouring a couple of pills in my hand.

I backed away. "No thanks. I kind of like the idea of radicals running around inside my body. Gives me that aggressive edge." I punched my fists out Rocky-style, like a boxer faking jabs.

"You might be sorry someday, Luke," she said. "Free radicals are nothing but trouble."

Chapter 5

My birthday was coming up. I was turning fifteen, oldest in my class. I used to bug Mom about it. "How come you held me back?"

"Everybody could use an extra year. I'd give anything to get one of mine back. Besides, you're growing up all too fast as it is," Mom said, hugging me.

I used to tell people I had missed the cut. But finally in about seventh grade it occurred to me that I did need more time, if only to get bigger for sports.

One night Dan and I went to the store after practice. I was hoping Amy would be there, and she was, arranging some fabric. She looked even better than before, with her hair pulled back in some kind of braid. Dan nudged me and raised his eyebrows when he first caught a look at her.

He immediately started asking Amy questions about her wheelchair, and it didn't seem to bother her at all. "Pretty cool, huh? It's got a turning radius of only seventeen inches, so much better than those old clunky ones they used to have." Right in the aisle she pulled a 360, and she was right. That baby could maneuver.

I hated to leave, but I figured I'd better check in with Mom. She sat working at her desk in the backroom. I picked up the newspaper and, not finding the sports page, glanced at the national headlines instead.

"Wow, twenty-seven years on the run. Did you read about this woman, Mom?" I stared at the two photos on the front page. Supposedly of the same woman, but they looked nothing alike, especially the hair. In one she was smiling with her husband and three daughters. In another she was dressed in camouflage gear, carrying a rifle and looking a lot younger.

"Mom?" She didn't answer me. I skimmed the article. "Sounds like she's been hiding as a PTA-mother type for twenty years. She's wanted for robbing banks for some radical political group before that. I wonder how the police found her?"

Mom seemed busy, so I headed back out to Dan and Amy. There were no customers around on such a warm night. "So you've been paralyzed ever since your car wreck?" I heard Dan ask.

"That's the story."

"I'm sorry."

"Don't feel sorry for me," Amy said. "I'm doing just fine."

I stopped and studied the button rack, trying to imagine what it would be like to have your life change in an instant. One minute you could walk and the next you couldn't.

Amy began rewrapping some red-flowered fabric on its cardboard holder. "I go swimming, play the flute, even go to dances." I walked up the aisle toward them.

Amy noticed me. "Hey, Luke, I've offered Dan here a ride home. Want one, too?" "Of course," I wanted to yell out, but my mouth wouldn't move.

"Go ahead, you big lunks," Mom said. I hadn't heard her walk up behind me. "I've got to finish some paperwork before I head home."

"Meet you out front in five minutes," Amy said, gliding away.

"Does she actually drive?" I whispered.

Dan shrugged. "The bigger question is, has any girl this hot ever offered you a ride?"

I just laughed. "Maybe her dad is picking her up."

It was nine P.M. but still bright as day outside. "Dan, how would you dance with a girl in a wheelchair, anyway?"

He punched me. "Why do you care, Big Guy?"

Just then a silver van pulled up and honked. Amy sat at the wheel.

"Smooth rig you've got here," I managed to say, as Dan opened the sliding door and hopped into the far back seat. The middle seat had been removed, leaving room to store her wheelchair. I had no choice but to sit in the front seat.

"You seem surprised," Amy said without smiling.

"Well, I, uh . . . didn't figure you could . . . I mean were old enough—" Dan yucked it up big time while I made a complete fool of myself.

Finally, Amy rescued me. "I missed a lot of school because of the accident, so I repeated fifth grade. Last month I turned sixteen and this was my birthday present, especially outfitted for me."

I leaned back on the leather bucket seat. "Some present."

"Hey, my father fought hard for all this. Thanks to him and this van, I finally feel like I have some freedom."

I couldn't help staring at her legs and then up at the gear shift.

"So you want to know how I run this thing? Watch." Amy put her left hand on a handle and squeezed it. "This controls the brakes." She moved her hand to another lever. "And this controls the gas. I use them instead of the foot pedals." Then she put her right hand on the black knob attached to the steering wheel at the two o'clock position and twirled it around. "This is the spinner knob. It allows me to steer the van."

I must have looked nervous, because she laughed. "You can trust me," she said, pulling out of the parking lot. "Right, Dan?" she called back. Dan nodded as if he drove with her every day. "Some people actually think these controls are safer than steering with two hands. In fact, the guy who fixed up this van for me said that in ten years most regular cars won't even use foot pedals."

The girl could really drive. There was so much to watch, I didn't say anything for a while. And I could stare at Amy all day, gas lever or no gas lever.

But then something occurred to me. "Did Mom help you get into the van out behind the store?"

"No, I can get in and out all by myself."

How could that be possible? I wondered.

"See that metal contraption on the floor? It's a lift. But we'll save that demonstration for another time."

Yes! There would be another time. I didn't let myself wonder why Amy would want to hang out with a younger guy like me.

Dan whistled. "All this must have cost a fortune."

"What's your dad do, anyway?" I never could keep my mouth shut, no matter how often Mom told me not to ask personal questions.

Amy didn't act bothered. "He's a lieutenant colonel in the Army. But, hey, he didn't pay for all this. The other guy's insurance company did."

"You certainly deserve it," said Dan as she pulled into his driveway.

"Thanks, Amy. Nice meeting you," Dan said, opening the door.

I got out too. "Hold on, Dan. Would you mind throwing around a bit? I'm feeling rusty for tomorrow night's game."

Dan hesitated, but I held his eyes. "Okay," he said, looking at me like I was crazy.

"Thanks for the ride, Amy. Great van." She rolled her eyes at me and waved goodbye. When she started pulling out of the driveway, I ran alongside and she braked to a stop. I leaned into the window. "Don't forget. You promised us a demo of your lift sometime." She nodded and continued backing out.

Dan started clucking and flapping his arms. I ignored him and instead watched Amy streak away. "You could have had her all to yourself." I didn't need reminding. "But that was a smooth move, running alongside her van."

"Shut up, Danny Boy. I didn't want you to think that I was hogging her." He snorted. "Come on. Throw me some balls. All Star tryouts are coming up."

We walked into Dan's backyard and grabbed a ball and a couple of gloves off the patio. "Hey, Luke," he said, tossing me a ball. "How come you didn't tell me how good-looking she was?"

"A guy has a right to a few secrets, doesn't he?"

"Sure. But I'm surprised you even took me by the store. I'm pretty hot with the ladies, you know."

Anybody would be hotter than me, I thought.

We threw for only a few minutes. Then we grabbed two sodas and sat on his lawn. "Did your dad ever play baseball?" I asked.

"I don't think so. It sure doesn't show in the advice he gives me." We both laughed.

"But he's built just like you, and you got your pitching arm from somewhere."

"I guess. I never seem to please him, though. I just wish he'd get off my back."

"At least you've got a father." Neither of us said anything more. We just sat there, swatting mosquitoes and pulling out blades of grass.

Chapter

I planned on having an awesome birthday game, especially with Sid home to see it. What a laugh. I popped out twice and when I struck out with the bases loaded, I threw the bat. Coach benched me. I looked over as Mom and Sid got into the car and drove off.

The problem was I wanted to show up Tim Crew, the smart-ass pitcher on the other team. He had needled me all year at school about what a fun time they'd had in Juneau at the Junior All Star state tournament. He and Lemming were the only first-year Junior players to make it.

Sid came back to pick me up. I got in the car and slammed the door. "We lost, 12–5. I might as well kiss All Stars good-bye."

"Maybe so," Sid said, "if you're going to keep playing like tonight."

"Our team is pathetic. Nobody can play."

I sat there fuming until Dan came over and dragged me out of the car. His mom had brought a cake so the team could sing to me. I kind of enjoyed the attention. Mom would never do something so public.

But she always made a big deal about birthdays at home, including a cupcake in bed when I woke up in the morning and whatever I wanted for dinner. That night I chose the fresh king salmon Sid had brought in from the village. Kathleen and Dan were joining us.

While Sid was barbecuing, Kathleen told the weirdest story about her mother's funeral the month before.

"My sisters and I went to the funeral home to sit with Mom's body for a while. But we couldn't find her, and there were no signs on the doors. We kept checking out the various rooms, but none of the bodies remotely resembled her. Finally we got the funeral director, and he showed us Mom laid out in her coffin. It was the right size body but the wrong face. It didn't look like her at all," she said, choking up.

"Talk about a bad makeup job," Kathleen added, laughing and crying at the same time and wiping away her black-streaked tears.

Mom patted Kathleen's hand. "Death is never easy." I looked at Mom and then at Sid. Was she thinking about my dad? Was my dad like Sid or had Mom chosen somebody completely different the second time around?

Dan started talking about Amy's hot car and everybody

laughed except Mom. "Amy is an incredible person. She doesn't want any special favors," she said, setting the table. "I'm glad we hired her."

"Yeah. Life in a wheelchair can't be easy," Dan said.

"And to think it could have been prevented," Kathleen added. "That fraternity boy should have been tarred and feathered."

"Some college party boy hit her? Was he drunk?" I asked.

Kathleen nodded. "She was riding to school on her bike."

That's why her family sued. "They must have so much money now, I'm surprised Amy needs to work."

"It's not that simple, Luke," Sid said, serving up the salmon.

"Of course it is. Somebody messes up your kid, you sue the daylights out of him."

"Money isn't going to give Amy her legs back," Mom said, her lips pinched together.

"A wrong's a wrong," I spit back, "and somebody has to pay." I stopped in my tracks and stared at Mom. "Did you ever think about suing when my dad was killed?"

Mom looked up startled, her face gone gray. "I—I—"

Kathleen said, "It was a different time back then, Luke. People didn't go to court as much."

"But it would have helped, Mom. I'll bet you didn't have much money when I was born."

"Speaking of being born," Dan said, "was Luke a hulk even at birth?"

I looked at Mom, but it was Kathleen who answered. "What a night. We were both waitressing at the Green Goddess restaurant, and Faith here was determined to work right up until Luke was born."

Mom smiled as Kathleen continued. "But then the labor pains started coming, right in the middle of the dinner rush. Tony, one of the dishwashers, had to drive Faith to the hospital while I covered the whole place myself." I'd never heard this story before. Nor thought about how lonely it must have been for my mom after my dad died.

"When we got to the hospital, Tony fainted," Mom added.

"You were so precious, Lukey," Kathleen said, pinching my cheek.

"Lukey?" Dan said, pinching my other cheek. I pushed away his arm.

Kathleen dug something out of her purse and handed it over to me. "Your baby picture." I stared at it.

Mom had frizzy black hair and looked real happy and young, even without my dad around. I'd never seen a picture of her, I realized at that moment. She never wanted one taken. Always said that she looked too fat or her hair was a mess.

Mom stood up. "Time for cake. Luke's favorite—chocolate with fudge frosting."

Dan, who was usually quiet around adults, kept asking questions. "So when did you two start the fabric store?"

"I convinced Faith to stay in Fairbanks. She was talking about going back to cook at a pipeline camp, where the money was good. But that was no life for a baby."

"I'm sure these boys aren't interested in ancient history, Kathleen."

"Then how about a more current scoop? When the Quilting Bee needed a whole new rewiring job, we sure got a good deal on Sid's services—after he laid eyes on Faith, that is."

Sid went over and kissed my mom. For so long it had just been the two of us. But I was glad that Mom had found Sid. Sid treated her great. But she never seemed happy. Had she never gotten over losing my dad? I thought she had. She never mentioned him.

Sid, Dan, and I played catch while Mom and Kathleen cleaned up. Later, when I went to the bathroom, I heard them talking in the kitchen. "Why did you hold on to that birth photo?" Mom asked.

"Luke has a right to know his history, Faith. When are you going to clue him in?"

"I haven't figured out the right time yet."

"To leave or to tell him?"

Tell me what? I wondered. But not enough to barge in and ask.

Chapter

When I got up the next morning Mom was still home, drinking coffee at the kitchen table. "You're going to take me for my learner's permit? I thought Sid was."

"He got called back to the village. Some emergency with the project."

"Damn," I muttered under my breath. "I thought he'd be home for a few days."

She shook her head and played with a napkin on the table. "Don't talk like that." She looked up at me. "Let's go backpacking on Angel Rocks."

"Yeah. After baseball season." I was stalling, hoping that by August she'd have forgotten all about it. "Come on. Let's go get my permit."

"That will be too late."

"Mom, they're open until four thirty and my game's not until six." I poured myself a bowl of cereal and sat down at the table. "Things slow at the store?"

"There's something I need to tell you."

When I didn't look at her, Mom grabbed the cereal box I had started reading. "I've been like one of my plants, my delphiniums in winter, lying under a pile of leaves, shut off from the world." Her voice sounded strange—soft and breathy. "I need to be uncovered. I need water."

"So do I," I joked, walking over to the sink and filling up two glasses of water. I couldn't help staring out the window at her garden.

She refused the water.

"Luke." She leaned across the table and took my hand. "There's something I've been hiding from you."

I felt the Cheerios make their way back up my throat. "Yeah. You dye your hair blond like half the women in America. You cheat on crossword puzzles—"

"Stop it." Her voice was shaking, worse than after that bomb scare at school, even worse than when she'd found out I'd stolen some comic books in fifth grade.

I stood up and dumped my cereal into the sink. "Mom, come on. You promised I could get my learner's permit today." I walked toward the doorway.

She didn't move except to put her head in her hands. Her voice was muffled when she started talking again. "My real name is Mary Margaret Cunningham. I grew up in Spokane, in a big Catholic family with three brothers and two sisters."

I grabbed the doorway with my hands. "What?" Her words couldn't seem to penetrate my brain.

"When I was a freshman in college . . . I helped set a pipe

42

bomb . . . in the ROTC offices at Berkeley, to blow up their records, as a protest against the Vietnam War."

I leaned to one side to hold myself up. After a few seconds I finally managed to say, "Lots of college kids did stuff like that."

"That war was horribly wrong and killed thousands of innocent people." She looked over at me, her eyes begging me to understand.

"Okay. But it was a long time ago, and it doesn't matter anymore." I walked over and tried to nudge her up out of the chair. "Come on, Mom. You've got a life here and now, which includes a new husband and getting your son his permit."

She threw off my arm and leaned forward, gripping her legs. "That bomb killed a student. I didn't mean to, Luke. Please believe me. I didn't mean for that to happen." She sounded like she was crying.

"Somebody died?" I grabbed the back of the chair.

"It was a month after the National Guard had killed those students at Kent State. The campus was practically deserted. Most of the students had gone home early for summer because Governor Ronald Reagan had shut down all the college campuses in California. He feared the protests and marches were getting out of hand. The bomb was set to go off at one o'clock in the morning. We had no idea that anybody would—"

I covered my ears and ran out of the kitchen. "I don't want to hear this," I yelled.

43

She followed me down the hallway. "Four of us were indicted for second-degree murder in absentia. I've been on the run from the FBI ever since."

"Shut up, Mom! I don't want to know any of this."

I went into my room and grabbed my baseball bag out of the closet. "What does Sid think of your hidden past? Where is he, anyway? He's never around when we need him."

"Luke, please," Mom said, clutching my arm. "The others have long since been caught or turned themselves in. Now it's my turn."

"Where's my catcher's mitt?" I dumped my bag upside-down on the bed.

"I'm going to California next month to turn myself over to the authorities. I was hoping you'd come with me."

I finally found my glove on the closet floor and stuffed it into my bag. "You've got to be kidding."

She tugged at my shirt as I walked out of the bedroom. "You need to understand how guilty I've felt all these years. No matter how hard I try, I can't seem to get over it."

"Well, try harder."

But she didn't. I walked along, getting soaked in the sudden rain and trying to convince myself that Mom was depressed, maybe even delusional. She needed counseling.

At the park some mothers and kids huddled under the picnic shelter, waiting out the storm. We used to spend every Sunday there. Mom would sit and read while I played myself out. She never left me alone, not even when I got older. How could she now?

Two old people sat at a picnic table in the shelter, watching their grandchildren play on the monkey bars in the rain. Did I have any grandparents? Did they know about me?

I had to get Mom to change her mind before she told the whole world.

I found her lying down on her bed, drapes drawn, eyes closed. She didn't answer when I whispered her name. I tiptoed inside her bedroom and watched as her chest moved up and down.

I went into my room and dug the paint grenade out of my underwear drawer and held it in my hand. I couldn't picture my mom setting a pipe bomb. Funny. You'd think the kid who loved toy guns, paintball, and violent movies would have thought her crime was cool. No. It was real life, some college kid's life, unless she made it all up. But why?

Last year on television there was this story about a twenty-five-year-old guy who went back to his old high school, pretending to be a student again. He accomplished everything he'd never done the first time around—straight A's, soloist in the choir, wide receiver on the football team— and nobody caught on.

It had been just another of his many cons since dropping out of school. The high school kids interviewed on the show said he'd duped them, used them, even betrayed them.

But he'd been their friend and given them good advice. He'd actually learned some things, too, and tutored other students. What was so wrong with what he did? I'd love to have an older friend help me through high school, somebody who knew about life but wasn't my parent. I could trust that he wasn't trying to protect me but instead was giving me the honest truth.

That's a good one—a con telling you the truth. I wondered what else Mom had lied about.

Eventually this guy ended up back in jail for some other crime. He told the interviewer, "Those kids thought I was something special. I'd never felt that way before. They helped me believe that being myself, the one who was mature and worked hard, was better than conning people."

So why were the kids mad? All he lied about was his age. All Mom lied about was her name. Okay. So I didn't know my relatives. There were worse things.

She was smart and tough, had outfoxed the FBI for thirty-one years. Like Mom said, she hadn't known that anybody would get hurt, let alone die. It wasn't her fault. People make mistakes.

On the way to the game I asked Mom not to tell anybody for a while. "Not a chance," she said. "I don't want the FBI showing up at the door before I'm ready to turn myself in."

I was surprised when she offered to drive me to the field and told her so. "Luke, I learned a long time ago that I couldn't just hide, that I had to have a life. But it's getting harder and harder. We'll talk some more after the game."

The phone was ringing when we walked in the door. I told Mom I didn't want to talk to anybody, not even Sid. A few minutes later she came in and sat on my bed. "Do you remember how on Thanksgiving and Christmas I would prepare a big dinner and then usually end up in bed with a migraine headache and a bout of depression?"

"I remember your great walnut and cranberry stuffing," I said into the pillow. "You just have a tough time with the cold and dark up here in the winter. Lots of people do."

She massaged my shoulders. "No. It's more than that, honey. I couldn't be with my family. I kept thinking that if I cooked for people I loved, everything would be all right."

I rolled over onto my back. "You always used to tell me that I was all the family you needed."

She walked over to my desk. "The best thing I ever did was to bring you into the world. During my years on the run I'd given up my family and all my friends. When I found out I was pregnant, I couldn't give you up, too. Having a baby was the one gift I gave myself."

She picked up one of my trophies.

"I had hoped my child would never have to know about the horrible wrong I committed or the life I left behind. I thought we could live in our own little world, that my love would be enough." She turned and looked at me, her green eyes searching my face. "But I'm finally learning that I can't control you, any more than I can control Sid or my feelings of guilt about causing a death." She put down the basketball trophy and started for the door.

I sat up in bed. "The second best thing you could do, Mom, is not turn yourself in. It isn't going to bring that kid back." When she didn't respond, I said, "Please."

"But the guilt is eating me alive, Luke." She leaned her back against the wall and closed her eyes. "I tried to bury it, push it down deep in my soul, but it always returns. I can't live like this anymore, and you deserve to know who I really am."

"I do know. You're my mother." I threw my pillow against the opposite wall and watched it fall.

After a while I knelt on my bed and pulled open the window blinds. "Are they still after you?" I asked, searching the street for unmarked cars.

She shook her head. "I've been off their Most Wanted list for probably fifteen years. As far as I know, my photo's not displayed in any post offices."

I tried laughing, but it came out a grunt. My mother's mug on an FBI poster. "Mom, the FBI couldn't find you. Not compared to that lady back East who didn't even try to disguise herself. It took a tip from a TV show to help track her down."

"I'm not worried about that, Luke."

"So why now? You and Sid just got married."

"I can do this now because of Sid." She walked back over

and sat on the bed. "Oh, honey. I can't live like this any longer. And I have to see my folks before they die."

"Have them come up and visit. It's safe here. Alaska is a great place to hide."

She leaned in to hug me. "Oh, Luke. If only that would do it."

After that, Mom was everywhere, showing up at practice, dragging me home from Dan's. I didn't want her going out. I couldn't let the FBI catch her before I convinced her to change her mind. Worried about her and not my playing, or anybody else's for that matter, I played my best ball of the summer.

Chapter 8

One night Kathleen drove me to my game. In the car she lit up a cigarette.

"I thought you were quitting."

She took a long drag and looked at me. Then she blew the smoke out slowly. "Some things are impossible to change."

"Like my mom's past?"

Kathleen looked at me funny and my heart jumped. She didn't know. I'd blown Mom's cover. Here I'd been so careful, not talking to anybody. Not even Dan.

"I'm glad she told you, Luke. You need time to process it."

"Why can't she just sneak down and see her parents in Spokane?"

I started punching my hand in my mitt. "Maybe if she'd told me earlier. Sid's known for a while. Why couldn't she trust *me*—instead of telling all those lies?"

Kathleen parked the car at the field and then grabbed the mitt out of my hand. "I just found out recently myself, Luke. Look at me. Would you really have wanted to know? I was hurt at first, too. But think of the pressure it would have put us under. She was trying to protect you, me, our business."

We won the game, 2–1, thanks to my double in the sixth inning, which drove Lemming home with the winning run. The victory brought our record to 11–9. So even if we lost our last game, we'd still have a winning season. Hardly the championship, but far better than last year's cellar ranking.

Afterward Lemming pounded me on the back. "Way to go, McHenry." Was that still my name? I wondered. "How about another round of paintball in the woods near my house?"

Splattering those balls would have been the perfect way to blow away the free radicals in my body. But then I saw Kathleen waving me over. Amy. Amy had shown up. She was sitting in her wheelchair next to the fence, her van parked on the street. I still couldn't believe a high school girl as good-looking as Amy would want to hang out with me. Was it just because most kids her age avoided her and her wheelchair?

"Sorry. I can't. A family friend's here."

"McHenry—" Lemming called.

I ignored him and walked over to the fence instead.

"You hungry, Luke?" Kathleen asked.

I nodded. "Always. Hi, Amy."

"Nice hit," she said, giving me a thumbs-up sign.

Kathleen opened her purse and handed Amy a twenty-dollar bill. "A going-away present. Get some dinner and take this big lunk along. The poor boy is starving."

We looked at each other, embarrassed. But it wasn't as if it was a date. Kathleen was insisting and paying for it, too.

Amy recovered first. "Great. Let's go to Skipper's. I've got a hankering for shrimp."

"A hankering? Where are you from, gal?" I sounded like an idiot. But Amy laughed, and suddenly I felt charming.

"You asked me earlier how I got into the van. Here's your demonstration." Amy rolled up along the right side of the van and pushed a button on the remote control attached to her key ring. The van door slid open. Then she pushed another button and this metal ramp unfolded from the floor of the van and stretched out, landing on the ground at an angle. Amy maneuvered her wheelchair and rolled up the ramp.

"Look inside, Luke, so you know the whole score." I ducked my head into the van. She punched the remote control again, and the ramp began folding back inside the van. I had to move to the side to avoid getting hit. With another click of the remote, the driver's seat dropped down and swiveled around. She moved from her wheelchair over into the driver's seat, using her arms. With daily workouts like this, no wonder she was so strong. Amy pushed the remote one last time, and the driver's seat swiveled back around and up to the steering wheel. Then she flipped a switch, which secured the wheelchair to the floor. Whoa. I was exhausted just watching.

"What are you waiting for, Luke?"

I hustled up front and into the passenger seat. We were on the road before I could blink. I looked over at Amy. From this view you'd never know she needed a wheelchair. Obviously neither did the guys who honked at her on Airport Road. No wonder Amy liked to drive so much.

"That remote is really something. It looks just like the one for Kathleen's car, but hers can't do tricks like this," I said, motioning around the van.

"Yup, it's pretty cool."

"What's this about a going-away present?"

Amy parked the van and turned off the engine. "We're leaving, sooner than expected. Dad's retirement request wasn't supposed to go through until late August. But surprise, surprise. That's the Army. We're moving back to California next week."

I changed out of my cleats, then stood around, wondering if I should offer to help. But Amy truly was self-sufficient. I actually felt kind of stupid watching her get out of the van. The only time I helped was with the door into the restaurant. "Ridiculous, isn't it? I get myself here but can't get through the door." I'd never noticed before how impossible it would be to open a door if you were in a wheelchair.

At the table I studied Amy while she looked around the restaurant. She wore a blue ribbed shirt. I wondered if she worked out with weights or if the wheelchair alone had toned her upper body. Whatever, she sure looked good.

"If you're one of those military brats who hate the cold, you must be happy to be getting out of here."

Amy looked up, frowning. "How can you say that with these incredible summer days that never end? Alaska wasn't my first choice. But now that we've been here a while, I'm going to miss it."

"Yeah? What about January? My mom is comatose then." Why did I mention my mom? She was the last person I wanted to talk about.

"Not winter. I certainly won't miss running my wheelchair over the ice." She finally smiled, her brown eyes lighting up. "But I will miss snow machining. That's what got me through."

"Really?" This girl was full of surprises. I'd ridden Dan's machine a few times but never gotten close to owning one. "Your family has one?"

She nodded. "Yours?"

Her family seemed to have everything. And Amy obviously didn't let her disability stop her from doing anything. In fact, she didn't have a "disability"; she had a special ability. I sat there, feeling pretty smart with that turn of phrase, and wondering if she'd feel offended or think I was clever if I repeated it to her.

"Earth to Luke." Amy leaned over and shook my arm.

"What? Did you ask me something?"

She had the deepest, darkest eyes, like pools of chocolate. "Yeah. I wondered if your family had a snow machine."

"My mom's not big on them."

Stupid. Why couldn't I get my mom off the brain? She sure wasn't worried about me.

Amy nodded. "If I was going to be here next winter, I'd take you out riding."

When I didn't answer, she started fiddling with the gold locket around her neck. "How is your mother?"

"She's fine." Did Amy know, too? How could she? "I hardly see her, being so busy with baseball."

"You played really well tonight."

"Thanks." I felt myself start to blush, but couldn't stop it.

The waitress put two glasses of water down on the table. "If you're here for the buffet, help yourself anytime."

"I can't," Amy said. "The buffet table's too high for my wheelchair."

The waitress placed two menus in front of us. "Maybe you'd like to order from the menu," she said uncomfortably.

"No, my friend can get me some food," she said, making her point oh so smoothly.

"How come they have it set up that way?" I asked, thumping down the saltshaker.

She shrugged. "You'd be amazed at the number of places I can't go—sidewalks without curb cuts, split-level homes, stores with narrow aisles."

"I never thought about that." She wouldn't even be able to get inside the front door of our house.

"People usually don't, unless it's their problem." She let out a sigh. "Hey, I didn't mean to spoil the mood. Why don't you just load up a plate for me with a little bit of everything?"

"This restaurant should lower the buffet table."

"Get me some food first, Mr. Crusader. I'm starving."

"Any chance you'll be able to walk again?" I asked, butter oozing out of my lips from the shrimp I had just bitten into. I tried to wipe it away with a napkin but ended up making a bigger mess.

Amy didn't seem to notice. "No. My spinal cord was completely severed. But at least I have the use of my arms. Some people aren't that lucky." She tried to sound positive, but her face didn't look it.

"I can't believe the driver who hit you was drunk." A hard knot started forming in the pit of my stomach. "I'd like to punch his lights out."

She didn't say anything for a minute. "It's history, Luke. The damage can't be reversed. But we can lobby for stiffer drunk-driving penalties. My parents and I work with MADD. You could come to a meeting sometime."

"Mothers Against Drunk Driving? But I'm not a

mother— at least, I don't think I am." I tried to laugh, but it fell flat.

"Forget it." She looked down at her plate.

"I'm sorry, Amy. I say the stupidest things sometimes." I picked at the potato salad on my plate. "My dad was killed by a drunk driver."

"I'm sorry, Luke. I didn't know that. I just figured your parents were divorced or something."

"He died before I was born, so it's not like I ever knew him or anything."

"But still . . ."

"So maybe I should volunteer with MADD instead of making fun of it."

Amy nodded. "It's funny. Your mom never mentioned it when I told her how I got injured."

"She never talks about my dad. It's like he never existed."

Amy stopped with her fork in midair. "Do you want to know more about him?"

I shrugged my shoulders. "So how did your accident happen?"

She didn't seem to mind my asking. "This college kid who had been partying all night was driving home, as I was biking to school. He ran a red light and plowed right into me."

"What a jerk."

"He wrote me a long letter of apology. He felt terrible."

"Oh, that's great. He apologized for ruining your life." Suddenly the knot in my stomach felt like it was exploding.

Had the driver who killed my dad ever apologized to my mom?

"He didn't ruin my life, Luke. But for a time I thought he had."

"I'll get us some dessert," I said, getting up.

Nothing looked good, but I brought back some chocolate cake and cheesecake anyway. "How come food never looks as appealing as in the commercials?"

"*Everything* seems better on television, even family fights," Amy said. "Maybe there's makeup for food, just like for models. They airbrush the food for the commercial, and reality can hardly compete."

We were quiet for a few minutes. "What if you hadn't biked to school that morning?" I said. "What if that frat boy hadn't been drinking?"

"I could drive myself crazy with 'what if's.' What if I'd taken another route? What if I had been sick that day and hadn't gone to school? What if the college student had left the party at midnight? Better yet, what if somebody had taken his keys away?" Amy drew designs with a knife on the tablecloth as she talked.

"Now my dad—he couldn't get over it. But thanks to his staying on top of the insurance company, I have a car and a snow machine specially outfitted for me. That's helped me leave my two-legged life behind."

When she dropped me off at home I said, "I'm sorry you're moving, Amy."

"Me, too, Luke. Good luck on the rest of your baseball season. Maybe you'll come to California sometime."

"Maybe." I waved goodbye and watched as she drove down the street. I wondered if I'd ever have a date with such a good-looking girl again.

Chapter

om had started going to church around Christmastime. That should have been a clue that things were changing with her. But I thought it was just because she was turning fifty and worrying about dying or something. Kathleen had turned fifty the year before and gotten really weird for a while. Personally I tried to avoid church as much as possible.

One Sunday in March I had agreed to go if she'd let me see a movie afterward. I was prepared to snooze. But the Catholic priest read the gospel story of the Prodigal Son in a booming voice that I couldn't tune out. As I listened, I sided with the older son. Why should his younger brother get to return home to this great party after blowing through his entire inheritance?

The priest paused and looked around. "What do you think would have happened if the father had refused to welcome his younger son home?"

The kid would have split again. But he didn't have any money.

The priest extended his huge arms and looked around, his beard bobbing side to side. "The father probably would have lost his younger son forever. Most of us have wasted our talents at one time or another or made a bad choice."

He walked down into the congregation and stopped near our pew. "Often the Prodigal Son story is misunderstood. We need to realize that both brothers made mistakes. The younger brother thought he had to earn back his father's love. The older brother thought he had to earn it in the first place."

The priest walked back to the altar. "God loves us unconditionally. He will forgive you, no matter what you've done wrong. Because like any loving parent he hopes you will learn and grow from your mistakes and most of all forgive yourself for being human. And after we accept that forgiveness for ourselves, we need to offer it to others in turn."

After mass Mom enticed me downstairs to the parish hall for doughnuts. What she actually wanted me to do was help at the soup kitchen. Before I knew it, I'd been handed an apron and was dishing up food for the street people.

I handed one guy his plate and he wouldn't let go of my hand. He kept staring me in the face, his filmy eyes crusted over. "Thank you so much, son," he said, his hand shaking.

Nobody had ever called me son. I wondered if he had any children and if they knew where he was.

When I walked into the storage room to put away my apron, I heard Mom talking to the priest. "Father, I haven't been to confession in years. Would you hear mine now?"

Mom never did anything wrong, I thought then. What a fool I'd been.

After our last game Coach pulled me aside and said I'd been nominated for Junior All Stars. I couldn't believe it. For four years I'd wanted to be one more than anything in the whole world. When I hadn't made All Stars in Majors either year and hadn't even been nominated for Junior All Stars last year, I'd been afraid it would never happen.

But this year they thought I was good. Coaches and kids actually thought I was a good player and had nominated me. It didn't matter what had happened other seasons or what Lemming or Crew said. This year I had a chance—if Mom kept undercover and if I continued to show what I could really do. Dan had been nominated, too, but I think he was more excited for me. That's the kind of guy he was. I always felt more selfish than him, always more worried about how I was playing, than how the team was doing.

Sid arrived home for his two-week vacation that same night. He and Mom had planned a halibut fishing trip to Homer and wanted me to go along.

"I can't leave now. Tryouts start Monday." I wanted Mom to get out of town, so she couldn't blow my chances.

"That's wonderful," Mom said, hugging me. "We'll stay around for moral support."

"No offense, but it didn't help before."

Her face fell.

"Did you just assume I wouldn't make All Stars again when you planned this trip?"

"That's not fair, Luke," Sid said.

"There's so much we haven't talked about, honey," Mom said.

"There'll be time when you get back." I gave her a kiss on the cheek. She looked surprised. I hadn't kissed her in a while. "I'm going to make it this time, Mom."

Sid followed me out onto the deck. "Luke, all three of us need this trip, to figure things out together."

"Sounds like it was already decided, long before this."

"It's what she wants, Luke, what she has to do."

"What about us, Sid?" I pounded the railing on the deck. "I want to make All Stars. What do *you* want?"

"I want your mother to be at peace."

"And you think leaving us and turning herself in will accomplish that?"

"Luke, we have to support her."

"Oh, yeah?" I kicked a loose deck board with my shoe. "Is that why you rushed back to work the day she finally told me?"

"You know that was an emergency. I wanted to be here." He kept talking, but his voice was shaking. "One Sunday a couple of months ago she'd been in our bedroom all afternoon, and I got worried. I found her sleeping, with the curtains pulled, *People* magazine flopped open on the bed. She'd been reading about a guy who found Jesus and then decided to turn himself in for raping a woman years ago, a crime his current wife had no idea about."

Sid leaned over the railing. I'd never heard him talk so much. A sentence was a big deal for him.

"Your mom told me everything before we got married. Said we couldn't have any secrets between us. She warned me that she needed to turn herself in when the time was right. That with me she had finally found someone she could trust to take care of you. I promised her I would, Luke. I promised her."

I turned away, wishing he didn't sound like he was going to cry.

The next morning I went to church with Mom, the first time since March. But when we arrived, I changed my mind. "I'll see if they need any help in the soup kitchen."

Downstairs I was surprised to see our neighbor Charlie setting out silverware and napkins. "I didn't know you helped out here."

"There's a lot we don't know."

I nodded. So true. I didn't get to serve any soup that day. Instead, I washed dishes with Charlie.

"Are some of those guys Vietnam vets? I've heard that a lot of the homeless are," I whispered.

He nodded. "That war messed up a lot of people."

———

That night I forced myself to say goodbye. "Have a good trip, Mom." She sat reading the Bible in the living room. We never even had one around until she started going to church. This whole mess had turned my mother into a Jesus freak.

"Thanks, honey," Mom said. "Good luck with tryouts."

"Could you pray that I make All Stars?"

"I'll pray that you do your best."

"Don't bother. Good night."

"Luke, wait. Jesus forgave a prostitute, of all people, and the Pharisees were shocked."

"Great. So now you're comparing yourself to a hooker."

She ignored that comment. Lately she hadn't gotten upset about anything. "Jesus told the prostitute that her faith had saved her. That's my name. Faith."

"No, it's a name you made up." Mom folded her hands and put them under her chin, then looked back down at her Bible.

"I like your name—Faith, Faith McHenry. I want you to keep it."

She nodded. "But I never should have been on the run all these years." She got up and walked over to the big picture window in our living room. "I had been raised to believe in a forgiving God. But after the bombing, I was so ashamed that I didn't think God, my parents, or Stephen Dolan's family could forgive me." She let out a long sigh. "They need to know that I haven't been a fugitive all these years because I didn't care that their son died or that I didn't think what we did was wrong."

"Mom, you talked to the priest. Didn't he say that God had already forgiven you?" I went over and tried to stare her down. "Why can't that be enough?"

Mom walked back over to the couch and picked up her Bible.

"Have it your way, Mom. But don't expect anything from me."

I moved over to Dan's the next morning. It wasn't until Sid and Mom were gone for a couple of days that I realized Mom had never left town before or left me. She and Sid hadn't even taken a honeymoon after their courthouse wedding last October.

Determined that these tryouts would be different, I didn't let myself think about the final outcome. I had the third fastest sprint time around the bases the first day. Dan pitched well, too. The coaches didn't have me playing catcher. But I didn't care. I'd take the outfield, I'd ride the bench. All I wanted was to make the team.

By the third day half the original forty players had been cut. Dan and I were almost there. Surprisingly there was a girl still in the mix—Michelle Kowalski. I had to admit that she was pretty good. But why she wanted to hang around with a bunch of crude guys, I had no idea. Of course, Crew and Lemming were in the running, too. I guess every new coach couldn't resist giving them a chance. Amazing how far talent can take you. Sid liked to say their lousy attitudes would catch up with them. I was still waiting.

I tried not to get my hopes up. Two years ago in Majors I'd gotten this far but then was scorched the last day.

Coach Stinson's parting words were, "If you don't get a call, show up at ten A.M. tomorrow." Dan and I stayed outdoors all night, far away from the phone.

The next morning Coach looked around at the fifteen players present and said, "Congratulations and welcome to the Junior All Star team."

Four years of disappointment melted away with that one sentence. I wanted to run around the field and whoop it up. I wanted to kneel down and thank God or the coach or somebody. But everybody else acted so cool, even Michelle. Probably because most of them had been on an All Star team before, some even to the state tournament. But not me. I felt like I was riding the biggest wave of my life with no spills in sight.

My last hit during batting practice I smacked a triple and tore around the bases. The coach yelled out, "McHenry, keep it up. That's exactly why I picked you for this team." Here I'd always thought I was better at fielding and running, but Coach Stinson thought I was a hitter—a power hitter. I didn't care what he called me as long as it was All Star. And as long as I kept playing, Mom wouldn't dare turn herself in.

When she and Sid returned from their fishing trip, I said, "Promise you won't leave until All Stars is completely over."

She didn't answer.

"Promise me."

She finally nodded.

If we could go all the way and win the state tournament, it would buy some time. Two weeks or more. Anything could happen in two weeks, right?

Chapter 10

It didn't take long to figure out that All Stars was a lot more pressure. Coach kept telling us that there'd be no guaranteed innings of play like in the regular season. At first I performed better with these kids who could actually play the game, as opposed to most of my Padres teammates.

But soon some of the guys started complaining in the dugout about the coach, the practices, and their positions. It spread to the field.

"It helps to catch the ball," Jake Aketachunak, the shortstop, yelled one day after I'd dropped a fly ball in center field. None of the Padres had ever dared put me down. I hated it and it began to affect my playing.

We needed some leadership. I could feel Coach and his assistants waiting, hoping one of us would step up to the plate. But neither Dan nor I could do it. I wasn't a good enough player, so the guys wouldn't listen to me. Dan needed to concentrate on his pitching, especially with Crew breathing down his neck. Nobody gave Michelle the time of day when it came to baseball, but they sure liked to flirt with her after practice, trying to outdo each other with their stupid jokes. Practices got more and more negative. I dreaded going. It showed in my poor play. I'd never felt that way before, even when Lemming had been at his worst and the Padres kept losing.

Lemming didn't act the same way on All Stars. He didn't dare if he wanted to play. He was actually the one who gave me the idea. He was bugging me to play paintball one night after practice. Other players overheard and wanted to come, even Michelle. "Why don't we go as a team?" I suggested to Coach Stinson.

Two days later the Fairbanks Junior All Stars pitted themselves against Military Madness. Lemming and I explained the rules. "Conserve your ammunition, stay alert, protect your teammates. The team with the last guy standing wins."

This time it would be fifteen teens against fifteen pilots. Our coaches decided to watch, like it was a practice or something. Those Air Force guys had six inches and fifty pounds on us, but the All Stars wanted it more.

The whistle blew and our team fanned out.

"Listen up, Blue," Lemming called out. "There's somebody at two o'clock." Sure enough, a Green came sprinting out of the woods, and we shot the hell out of him. Down he went.

More Greens started coming, and we Blues kept shooting.

"This sucks," Crew grunted as he got hit in the bunker below me. "I'm a dead man. McHenry, you shoulda had a line on him. Go after him."

Popping up, I nailed the enemy. Right in the groin, then ducked behind a boulder where Aketachunak crouched.

"Argh . . ." Green yelled out. His teammate came darting out in revenge, firing straight at me. *Splat.* Aketachunak zapped him in the forehead.

"What the hell . . . I'm going to get you, kid." Aketachunak and I started laughing. "Too late, big guy," Jake yelled.

"This is a blast," he said. "Why didn't you tell me before?"

"Lemming talks about it all the time."

"Lemming." Aketachunak rolled his eyes.

"Yahoo!" one of the Air Force crazies yelled out, tearing across the field. "I've had enough of you ball boys," he hollered. Dan hit the sucker right in his leg.

We blasted them for two hours, winning three games out of four. As a last-ditch effort, the pilots suggested we play Medic.

"We can beat you at anything," Lemming taunted.

Medic is a far more complicated game than Capture the Flag. If a player gets shot, he can get back in the game if his team's medic touches him. So the medic has to be fast and sneaky and his team has to protect him. "McHenry as medic," Aketachunak called out. "He knows how to make the moves." The others agreed.

Sweating like crazy, I crisscrossed the field. Under the

protection of my teammates I kept bringing my fallen comrades back to life. And I didn't have to shoot. Mom would have approved.

The Greens shot me halfway through the first game. "Our medic's down!" Lemming screamed as I lay there, orange paint splattered across my chest. I closed my eyes and felt like I was dying.

"The game's over without McHenry," Lemming yelled.

After paintball, the complaints pretty much stopped. We had learned to depend on each other. We were ready for anything.

One night after practice when Mom was late picking me up, Michelle and I talked for a while. "How can you stand playing with these cocky guys?"

Michelle looked at me, surprised. "Because I love baseball, real baseball. The speed is so different from the fast-pitch softball most girls play. It's not like I think I'm better than them, I just don't like softball as well."

"But hardly anybody gives you credit on the team. They might want you for a girlfriend, but not as a teammate."

"Says who?" She glared at me, then swatted my arm with her mitt. "No matter what, it's worth it. My mom tried to talk me out of it a couple of years ago, but my dad understood and encouraged me to stick with it. I loved the paintball. Didn't I hold my own?"

I didn't remember even noticing Michelle that night.

I looked at her. "Kowalski, you're actually not half bad.

Maybe even good enough to get some playing time in the outfield."

"Well, thanks a lot, McHenry," she said, patting my back. "Maybe you'll get to play, too." Just then her dad pulled up and she ran to the car.

"Wait, Michelle . . . I didn't . . ."

She waved as they drove off. What was it with me and girls? I could never seem to say the right thing. She was pretty good for a girl. No, she was pretty good, any way you looked at it. Maybe good enough to take my spot.

Coach issued us these fancy navy-and-white uniforms with real wool hats, instead of the ugly polyester ones we wore in the regular season. I spent some of my allowance money on a warmup jacket with "McHenry" stitched across the back.

Mom kept dragging me to appointments—doctor, dentist, haircut—even though I tried to get out of them. One night she asked me to get out my high school class schedule, but I pretended I couldn't find it.

One day she forced me to go shopping for school clothes. On the way home, she started talking about her dad and his blue seersucker suit. First religion, now Alzheimer's. It was scary.

"You never see men wear them anymore. But, boy, did he look handsome in his. One summer night he came home with a Hula Hoop, the latest fad. He twirled it round and round his waist." She started laughing. She never laughed. Was this how Mary Margaret Cunningham acted?

Finally it was tournament time. For once in my life I wanted the practices to go on forever.

I couldn't believe the hoopla at the district tournament. Before the game the announcer called out our names over the loudspeaker, just like in the real major leagues. Just like I'd always dreamed.

We won our first game easily against Delta Junction, 10–2. Everybody got to play. Two nights later we played Fort Wainwright and beat them, 5–2. After the second victory I couldn't sleep because next up was North Star, the other Fairbanks area team. If we beat them, we'd win district and a berth in the state championships. And if we kept winning, Mom stayed home.

I started sweating before the North Star game even started. All along we'd figured they'd be our toughest competition. I was so nervous warming up that I almost wished Coach wouldn't start me. He did, in center field right next to Michelle in left field. Crew pitched a solid first inning and scored our first run.

As the game went on, we scored, but North Star kept coming back: 1–2, 3–2, 4–3. In the bottom of the sixth and final inning, we were tied at 5–5.

Dan, who had been brought in as the relief pitcher, hit an easy fly ball for the second out. Then I was up, two outs, nobody on base. My legs felt like jelly, even worse than the morning Mom had told me her secret. I wasn't even sure I could get myself to the plate. Michelle came up to me. "Ice water," she said.

"What?"

"Pretend you have ice water in your veins. That's how the pros do it."

I walked over and stood frozen in the batter's box. But I soon went into meltdown, swinging at the very first pitch. Stupid—but I eked out a single because my speed beat the throw to first. With my head screwed back on, I stole second, and when Tim Crew hit a double off the now-rattled pitcher, I brought home the district championship.

After I touched home plate with the winning run, I turned around and waved at Mom and Sid. Mom was standing and clapping in the bleachers. I couldn't remember the last time I'd seen her sit with the crowd. Michelle and Dan were pounding me on the back. Lemming and Crew started to pick me up, but I fought them off. Nothing mattered but the victory, and the whole team had made that happen.

At our first state tournament game we all had a case of nerves, but we managed to beat Ketchikan anyway, 6–4. The next night Juneau handed us our first loss in postseason play, topping us, 7–5. The double-elimination tournament allowed us to bounce back, and we did, outlasting Kenai, 4–3. Two days later we got our revenge on Juneau.

Tied 1–1 in games against each other, we had to face Juneau one more time. If we beat them, we'd win the state championship and a ticket to the regional tournament. I wanted to win so badly, I lay in bed the night before just waiting for the devil to show up so I could sell my soul.

He never did, and the next day neither did my hitting. Cold. Oh, so cold. And I wasn't the only one.

At the top of the fifth the score remained 0–0, a great defensive game. Coach waved me over. "McHenry, you always shake things up. Just make contact. Then take the green light and steal, steal, steal." Somebody had to score, and Coach thought I had the magic.

At the last moment Juneau brought in a new pitcher. While he warmed up, I had plenty of time to think over all the batting advice I'd ever been given. One coach had told me, "Never swing at the first pitch."

Another had said the opposite. "Catch them off guard by sometimes taking that first ball." It had worked at the district championship. Against Juneau that day I let pitch after pitch sail by until the count stood at 3–and–2. Anything was possible—a walk, a strikeout, a home run.

As the next pitch came hurtling toward me, I waited for the perfect moment, then swung, expecting the sweet crack of success. Silence.

"St—r—iii—ke three!" screamed the ump. Not the hero that day. I felt like crap. I'd let the team down.

But Lemming was up next. Grinning, he strutted to the plate as if he were Barry Bonds. He hit like him, too. His double jump-started the team. Now I was the one screaming. We scored three runs that inning, two the next; and Crew ended up pitching a perfect game. I had to love the guy now. We had romped over Juneau, 5–0. We were the state champs! I'd never known I could feel so good.

At the pizza party afterward Coach stood at the head of the table. "I knew you could do it—I sensed it from the first day of practice. This time next week we'll be playing at the regional tournament in San Jose, California!" he shouted, his arm punching the air. The whole team started pounding the table in unison.

California? Before this I hadn't let myself even think about the next level. California?

"Where's San Jose?" I asked Dan, leaning across the table.

"Just below San Francisco."

"Near Berkeley?"

"Sorta. Other end of the bay. My cousins live in Santa Cruz," Dan hollered over the noise, "so it's perfect for me."

I felt sick. My first trip outside Alaska, and I was headed for Mom's criminal backyard.

Chapter 11

"Congratulations, Luke," Mom said later that night, when she came in to say good night. "I guess it was meant to be. We can watch your tournament, and then I'll turn myself in." She said it slowly, as if our victory was a sign that she was doing the right thing. "Maybe your grandparents could even catch a game."

"That's crazy. Your parents don't even know I exist." I threw off my sheet. "It's you they want to see, if you're lucky and don't get arrested in front of my team and ruin my life, along with yours." I punched the wall, so hard I almost put a hole in it, like I had in sixth grade. "You're not going. Not now. This is my time, Mom. I've been dreaming of this night ever since I was a little kid. We're state champions. You're not going to screw it up."

She started crying and left the room. I tried to go to sleep, but I couldn't. When I got up to watch some television, Mom was still up, sitting on the couch with Sid. I stood and listened from the hallway. "I shouldn't have told Luke what I was planning. He's right. It's his night and I've ruined it."

I walked into the living room. "You're right. So cancel your plans." I was calm, the anger faded. "At least until after school starts. Dan's family can look out for me down at the tournament. Just stay here."

She looked up at me. "It's too late, Luke. Last week my California attorney negotiated a plea bargain for me."

"No." I kicked the chair leg. "Without you being there? That's not possible."

"Ron Blake, my attorney here in Fairbanks, located a terrific lawyer who was able to handle the whole thing anonymously. She realized how important it was for me to turn myself in after an agreement had been reached."

"And as usual I'm the last to know."

I glared at Sid as he got up and left the room. "So they don't know who you are or where to find you?" She nodded her head. "Then wait until I graduate from high school."

"Luke, this plea bargain guarantees me a six-year sentence. Six years under the California system translates to only two years in jail, with four years off for good behavior. And believe me, I will behave." She laughed the fakest laugh. I felt like my chest was burning up.

She let out a sigh. "I'll be home in two years, in time for your junior year of high school." She tried to smile, but the sides of her mouth twitched instead.

Watching her face, it finally registered, like an echo coming from the other side of a canyon. "Jail?" I grabbed a pillow off the couch and threw it across the room. "You're going to jail? I thought you'd just go down there and they'd slap your hand. I thought the big deal was the embarrassment, the humiliation we'd all be put through. How could you possibly agree to go to jail? Those places are horrible."

"Luke, someone died in the explosion. I'm sorry. I thought you understood all this."

"How could anybody understand this stupid mess?" I stared out the living-room window, then turned back to her. "Wait. I thought the FBI was looking for you. Aren't they the feds? Why do you have to go to California to turn yourself in? Couldn't you do it anywhere, like here?"

"The FBI was looking for me. The use of explosives and fleeing over state lines are both federal offenses." She began twirling her wedding ring, round and round. "But the bombing took place in California, so thirty-one years ago I was charged by both the feds and the state of California. So technically I can surrender myself to either. Apparently the feds are swamped right now, so they're happy to drop their charges after all this time and let the state of California handle it."

"Happy?" I sat down beside her on the couch. Mom wouldn't look at me.

"Actually Diane Winston, my attorney, said how lucky I am that the state of California is willing to negotiate it. Their system of sentencing is much more lenient. The feds have mandatory sentences and offer no time off for good behavior."

"Good behavior. Jail. Whatever you say, Mom." Funny. Somehow I had thought it was all talk and that in the end she wouldn't go through with it.

Mom put her arm around my shoulder. I didn't shrug it off. "Remember how we tried to pick blueberries last summer and there weren't any? But this year the conditions are perfect, just enough rain and sun to produce a bumper crop."

"Who cares about blueberries?" I pulled away. "You're losing it, Mom."

"The conditions are right for *me* now, too, Luke. Remember how the priest talked about the Prodigal Son and forgiveness? Well, it's time for me to ask for it."

I picked up my Nerf ball off the carpet and threw it against the window—the ball I'd been tossing around since I was a little kid. Forgiveness. Berries. Funny, Kathleen was always talking about how great blueberries were for protection against free radicals.

I used to love to pick blueberries. Leaning down and sticking my hand into those red leaves, I'd drink in that ripe, sweet smell. I never could resist popping a few into my mouth, the seedy skin pushed against the roof of my mouth and the soft, fleshy insides sliding down my throat.

I went to my room and tried to pack, banging drawers open and closed. But I couldn't find anything I needed, except my paint grenade. Mom came and stood in my doorway, and I just got confused all over again.

"There are some things we should talk about, Luke.

You're going to need a guardian while I'm gone. If Sid adopts you—"

"Leave me alone, Mom. You're doing what you want. Let me do the same."

"Let him pack, Faith," Sid said, walking up behind her.

"Sid," I said, "you're just going to sit back and let this happen?"

He didn't say a word, didn't even blink an eye.

"No matter what you're feeling right now, Luke, we have to prepare you," Mom said in a quiet voice. "Ron said the national media could pick up the story and—"

I tried to laugh, but it came out like a grunt. "Here I'd dreamed of being featured in *Sports Illustrated* someday. But no. Now I'm going to be famous as the poor, deserted son of the fugitive Mary Jane—"

"Mary Margaret Cunningham."

"What is so wrong with us and your life here that you have to give it all up? And why now? Just so you can turn the best time of my life into the worst? Does that make you happy, Mom?" I heard my voice shaking and tried to lean into the dresser to pull myself together.

"We'll get through this, Luke," Sid said. "But we gotta stick together."

"No, Sid. It's too late. We lost the game."

The next morning the phone rang, but nobody picked it up. I heard the answering machine kick in. "Luke, it's Dan. What are you taking on the trip? Call me back."

A few minutes later Mom walked into the kitchen. "Luke, I've decided we should have a little party tonight. Why don't you call Dan and invite him?"

"A party? And just what is there to celebrate?"

"A going-away party for both of us."

Mom never had parties. She once told Sid that if he ever gave a surprise party for her, she would turn around and leave. Everything was different now.

I slammed the kitchen cupboard. "You already ruined my baseball celebration, and nobody celebrates going to jail."

About five o'clock I holed up in my room and logged onto the computer. Finally a message from Amy. She'd been gone three weeks and no word before this.

```
To: "Luke McHenry" <slugger@polarnet.com>
From: "Amy Stanton" <astanton@hotmail.com>
Subject: On the move


We made it! Sorry it's taken so long for
me to write. Moving is a nightmare, even
though I've been through it a million
times. It seems so crowded down here in
the Bay Area, compared to little ol'
Fairbanks. How did the baseball tournament
go? Write back soon.

Amy
```

It sounded like she might live near our baseball tournament in San Jose. I hit the reply button.

To: "Amy Stanton" <astanton@hotmail.com>
From: "Luke McHenry" <slugger@polarnet.com>
Subject: Coming to California

So you have survived and lived to see the
day in crazy California. The tournament
was awesome. We actually won, and I'm
coming to San Jose tomorrow. Finally a
trip out of Alaska and into the big, bad
world. Any chance you live nearby and we
could get together? You could show me the
sights in that hot van of yours. I'm so
glad you e-mailed me before I left. I sure
hope you read this tonight. E-mail me your
phone number and I'll call you when I get
in. Hurry!

Luke

I was tempted to tell her about Mom. I had to tell somebody, just to let the pressure off. But Amy would know soon enough, and you couldn't trust the Internet. The question was, could you trust anybody?

I sent the message off and then thought about entering a chat room and sharing my predicament with some anonymous person. But as I sat there, I wondered if I really wanted to share my mom's story with some possible weirdo on the web. Then I heard Mom's voice filter down the hallway. "So thirty-one years ago I protested the war, just like some of you, except—"

I slammed the door and logged onto a search engine instead, typing in *San Francisco Chronicle*. Okay, Mom. Since I guess there's no turning back now, let's see what actually happened.

I zipped right onto their website. On the right-hand side was a listing with all sorts of categories. I opened "Archives," thinking about how easy it was to find old issues of a newspaper.

But the website featured only editions starting in 1995. Now what? I tried some of the other sites listed on the search engine, but they all just featured info about San Francisco. On a good day I would have been all over them, finding out stuff about where I was headed tomorrow. But right then, I wanted some answers, not color photos of the Golden Gate Bridge or the cable cars. I thought about calling the library, but the phone was in the kitchen. Besides it was probably closed.

A knock on the door. "Can I come in, slugger?"

When I didn't answer, Kathleen knocked again and poked her head in. "You okay?"

She walked over to me and studied the computer screen. "What a great idea. Getting a head start on your sightseeing. I love the Golden Gate Bridge."

"Do you want to know what I was really doing?"

She nodded.

"I was trying to find some information on the Internet about Mom's bombing, but it's too long ago."

"I guess great minds do think alike." Puzzled, I watched as she pulled something out of her pocket. She gave it to me, her hand shaking a little.

I slowly unfolded a paper and looked at the banner: *San Francisco Chronicle*—Monday, June 1, 1970. "Where did you get these?" Saliva was collecting at the back of my mouth. I tried to swallow but couldn't.

"When your mother told me a couple of weeks ago, I wanted to know more, too. The library ordered microfiche copies of the newspaper for me, and they arrived yesterday. I sat at the library all afternoon today, loading that damn machine and trying to read the fuzzy copy."

I glanced at the headline but the words were blurry. I closed my eyes. When I opened them again, I still couldn't focus. Kathleen grabbed my shoulders and leaned in. Finally my eyes started moving down the page.

SDS SUSPECTED IN ROTC BOMBING

Police suspect the Students for a Democratic Society (SDS) in an early-morning explosion at the Reserve Officers Training Corps (ROTC) offices in Harmon Gym at the University of California Berkeley. A three-inch pipe filled with black powder blew up a file cabinet and a wall, killing student Stephen Dolan instantly. . . .

I pointed to the photo of the kid in a military hat and read the caption. "Stephen Dolan." I put the paper on the desk. "He looks like a nice guy, Kathleen, like a kid playing soldier. Why did he have to be in those offices that night?"

Kathleen shook her head and started pushing her cuticles back. "I protested the war that spring of 1970, too. All I did was march around carrying signs and singing songs. But I wanted to do more. So many of us felt frustrated by the brutal, futile fighting. Guys I grew up with were getting killed, Luke, for nothing. Your mom's not crazy. Yet it always seems to come down to this—should you use violence to stop violence?"

Kathleen walked over to my window and stared out. "One evening I had the flu and was lying on the couch in my apartment watching television. On came the newsreel of the National Guard throwing tear gas into the crowd and killing four students at Kent State."

Kathleen looked like she had the flu now. Her voice had dropped so low I could barely hear her. "I was going to school at the University of Indiana. A group of us drove over to Kent State in Ohio for the memorial service." She turned back toward me. "I think that tragedy did more to end the Vietnam War than fifty-eight thousand dead American soldiers."

Later I lay in bed, trying to sleep. I didn't want to think about war and killing and dying. America wasn't fighting a war right now, but racists were killing people in schools, churches, and office buildings. Would I do something radical to stop them?

I was sticking with baseball. At least you always know the score and whose team you're on.

Chapter 12

When I woke up the next morning, I checked my e-mail first thing. With our team scheduled to leave at midnight on the red-eye special, I'd been hoping that Amy checked her e-mail every day, because I had only twelve more hours to hear from her. There she was right on the money.

To: "Luke McHenry" <slugger@polarnet.com>
From: "Amy Stanton" <astanton@hotmail.com>
Subject: Wow!

I can't believe you're coming down. How
wonderful that your team won the tournament. You worked hard for it. Please stay
a few extra days if you can. I'd love to
show you around. My parents are thrilled
because I've been bored to death, waiting

for school to start. My phone number is
(825) 555-8124. Call the minute you get
in. I want to come to your games, too.
Later, 'gator.

Amy

Yes.

To: "Amy Stanton" <astanton@hotmail.com>
From: "Luke McHenry" <slugger@polarnet.com>
Subject: Double wow

I can't believe it either. Not sure if I
can stay but would like to. I will call
you when I get in, and we'll make a plan.
I'm staying at the Howard Johnson in Santa
Clara. I am buzzed.

Luke

Her message kept me jazzed for an hour or so. But then I
just rattled around with nothing to do. Mom and Sid had
left without telling me where. Probably afraid I'd go off on
them again. A note would have been nice.

At one o'clock I turned on the television and watched the
credits roll for *The Young and the Restless*. A sour-faced girl
flashed on the screen, standing in a rich mansion, speaking

to her mother, who wore a fancy silk bathrobe. A far cry from Mom's beat-up one.

"He's my father? You mean, all these years you've been lying about *kind* Uncle Jack? How dare you keep something so important from me, Mother. I had a right to know."

I shut off the tube. My life was a soap opera. Mom had lied all these years about her real identity. Had she lied about my dad, too?

I made Kathleen drive me to the airport, even though Mom insisted it would look strange if she wasn't there to say goodbye.

But nobody even noticed, not even Dan. He did ask me where I'd been the last couple of days.

"Family stuff." Stupid, open-ended answer.

"I know what you mean. My mom threatened to have me arrested if I didn't clean my room."

That's all I needed. Mom arrested in front of the entire team. They called our flight, and I was just about to board the plane when I noticed Mom walking toward me.

Loudly she said, "Luke, I'm so glad I got the chance to say goodbye. Our business meeting ended earlier than expected." I let her hug me. It occurred to me later that nobody has business meetings at midnight. What a lousy liar she was. No. She'd been lying quite well for thirty-one years.

Sid came running up, out of breath.

"I had to park the car." He shook my hand and said, "Knock 'em dead or better yet, out of the ballpark." Mom and Sid were both smiling, like they'd really pulled something off. Until these two men dressed in jeans and plaid shirts—that's what everybody thinks Alaskans dress like—interrupted us.

"Excuse me," the tall, skinny one said to my mom. "Do you know this man?"

Mom drew in her breath and calmly put her arm through Sid's. "Why, of course. He's my husband."

"Just asking, ma'am. We're the FBI—" I felt my eyes go to the back of my head. Somebody pulled my arm and led me to a chair.

"Luke. Luke. You okay?" Kathleen's voice sounded far away.

"I, I—"

"Last call for flight 485, departing for Seattle and San Francisco."

I stood up and walked over to Mom. The man was still talking to her. "Sorry to scare you, ma'am. Lots of drug trafficking going on up here. Yes, even in little ol' Fairbanks, and they told us to question any suspicious parties. This husband of yours," he laughed, tapping Sid on the chest, "looked awfully nervous, parking his truck and running into the airport. We just thought we'd better check it out."

Dan called across the waiting area. "McHenry, they're going to leave without us."

"Mom—"

"Goodbye, honey. I love you."

I nodded and ran to the gate.

As the plane taxied down the runway, I stared out the window. The FBI in Fairbanks? Looking for drug runners . . . or an old fugitive? At that very moment Mom could be under arrest. I felt helpless. No way to find out and nothing I could do about it.

Needing a distraction, I looked around, expecting the team to be getting rowdy or at least trading around comic books. But they were all settling down to sleep, parents and players.

I couldn't sleep. I just sat there in the darkened plane, thinking. Mom could ruin her life. But I wasn't going to let it ruin mine.

I had something special, playing on a winning All Star team after all those years of wanting it so bad. Some people never even get close to an experience like that. They never make a team, or get decent grades, or even have a friend they can trust.

I must have dozed during the flight to Seattle because I barely remembered our layover there. I didn't really wake up until the sound of the flight attendant's voice blaring over the intercom, "We are now preparing for our descent into San Francisco."

"Luke, look." Dan pointed down to a huge structure poking out of the clouds. "Pac Bell, the Giants' new ballpark." The whole team was awake now.

"Down there on the bay. Man, check out all those rigs,"

Dan yelled. All sizes of boats, from luxury yachts to tiny sail-boats, dotted the water.

"How do you know all this?" I asked.

"I've been down here before, remember? Besides, if you watch the Giants play on TV, they always pan in on the stadium and the boats out in the bay."

"Hey," said Aketachunak, "I heard loads of them just sit out there in the bay during a game. The people on the boats hope that one of the players will hit a home run over the wall and into the water. But it's only happened six times this season."

"I'll bet they've all been by Barry Bonds," said Lemming. "He's their only decent player." Lemming would favor Bonds. Both of them had big egos along with their big bats.

I turned around and called out, "Hey, Lemming, are you trying to say it takes only one player to make a team?"

Lemming frowned at me. "Everybody knows Bonds is the only reason the Giants ever win."

Dan looked at me as if to say, why bother even talking to that guy?

"Hey, Coach, are the Giants in town? Are we going to get to see them play?" Aketachunak asked.

"They are," I chimed in. I'd always wanted to see a major league baseball game. But no team more than the Giants. I followed every game.

The lights came on and everybody started moving around. While Dan looked for his shoes, I stared down at the rows and rows of houses all crammed together.

The flight attendant's voice broke through the chatter. "Please remain in your seats until we have safely arrived at the gate and the airplane has come to a complete stop." All around us passengers were getting up and gathering their things.

No one listens to authority anymore. Why should I? I thought. I nudged Dan up out of his seat; we crowded the aisle.

The airport was huge—ten, twenty times bigger than the one in Fairbanks. After we got our bags, Coach informed us, "You won't believe the day we've got planned for you."

As our two vans headed toward the freeway, a huge stone statue of the Madonna stared down at me. It looked like the statue at the church Mom had dragged me to in Fairbanks, only much bigger, like everything else down here. I looked up at Mary and begged, *I'm not religious, but I hope you'll help me anyway. Please don't let my mother leave Alaska.*

The freeway was jammed with cars, and we were barely moving. I felt like I'd landed on another planet. In Fairbanks we had two main highways, and most of the state didn't even have roads. But we had tons of animals. Down here the place was packed with buildings, roads, and people. No room for any animals.

"Are we in San Francisco?" I asked.

"We're getting there," Coach said. "Just passed through San Bruno, I believe."

"But how do you know where one town ends and the other begins?"

A couple of guys laughed, but most of them seemed to agree.

"McHenry, you've got to watch the road signs or life will pass you by," Coach said.

The city of San Francisco blew me away, with its tall buildings jutting into the sky and rolling hills. But the best part was the Golden Gate Bridge. It looked even better than on the Internet. As Coach drove across it, he told us about the painting crews who worked around the clock to make sure the bridge stayed bright and shiny. "Just like you guys have got to be—on your toes the whole time. Never letting up, no matter what the score." Just like Mom, thirty-one years on the run.

We ate shrimp cocktail along Fisherman's Wharf and visited Madame Tussaud's wax museum. John Wayne stood there in a cowboy outfit, Elvis with his guitar, Babe Ruth with a bat. They looked so real, I felt like I could talk to them. But of course they weren't. If the lights got too hot, they would melt.

We stopped to hear some street musicians. "Oh, they're just a bunch of hippies," Crew muttered.

"This is where they started, you know," his mother said. "Right here in San Francisco, in the Haight-Ashbury district." She frowned, her voice disapproving.

"Drugs and free love," Lemming said, laughing. "Sounds great to me."

Nobody liked hippies anymore. Mom was going to be

dead meat. She had lived right in this city and gone to the University of San Francisco, some Catholic college that her dad had chosen.

She had never attended classes at Berkeley, she had explained at some point when I was willing to listen. "But Berkeley was where the real protests were happening, so I started going to SDS meetings over in Berkeley."

If she had lived around here somewhere, I figured, she was probably into the drug scene. Maybe "under the influence of drugs" could be her legal defense. She sure didn't use them now. Didn't even keep aspirin or Pepto-Bismol in the house.

We pigged out on sourdough bread and chocolate sundaes at Ghirardelli's. When we rode the cable car, we all leaned out as far as we could until the conductor yelled at us.

"Next on the agenda, Alcatraz," Coach announced. Everybody cheered but me.

Alcatraz was the last place I wanted to go.

Chapter 13

Welcome to the Rock," a huge guy yelled as we pulled up to the Alcatraz dock, about a mile across the bay from San Francisco. With greasy black hair and built like a truck, he looked like he could have played on the line for the San Francisco 49ers forty years ago. He sounded just like the Sean Connery character in the movie *The Rock*.

The real Alcatraz didn't look nearly as exciting as the one shown in movies. It was just a rocky little island with broken-down buildings and weeds growing everywhere. I wanted to turn around and get right back on the boat, but the rest of the team, including our coach, acted like it was the best thing since Play Station.

"Okay, team," Coach explained, his voice cranked up a notch. "We have our choice of the general tour or a specialty one featuring Alcatraz escapes."

"Escapes," they all yelled. Nobody noticed my silence.

"Where are you folks from?" the park ranger called out, gathering a big group around him. He had long hair pulled back in a ponytail and looked like he could have been a hippie in Haight-Ashbury. I wanted to go up and ask him what he was doing during the Vietnam War, but he would have thought I was nuts.

"Alaska," Dan called out. Even he was into it.

The ranger whistled. "Long way to travel. Did you know that's where Robert Stroud was finally captured? Better known as the Birdman of Alcatraz, Stroud didn't actually keep any birds here. He did that during his stay at the federal prison in Leavenworth, Kansas." The ranger stopped and looked around. "And in real life he wasn't nearly as endearing as Burt Lancaster in the movie."

"What did the Birdman do to get locked up here?" an older man asked.

"Among other things, he killed a man in a barroom brawl in Juneau, Alaska."

"Juneau's not Alaska. They're just wimps with a little rain to deal with," Crew called out. "Not like our fifty-below winters in Fairbanks. Now *that's* Alaska." A few men in the group whistled. Our team just laughed. Juneau hadn't wimped out, but we beat them when it counted.

"I take it you boys are from Fairbanks. What are you doing down here?"

Sampson answered. "We won the state Junior Little League baseball championship, so we're representing Alaska at the regional tournament in San Jose." The crowd applauded.

"Good luck, guys," the ranger said, smiling. "Ready to hear some escape stories?"

"Whoo, whoo," we chanted. If I didn't think about Mom, I could actually have fun.

"Some hard-core criminals in prisons across the country just didn't want to serve their time and were quite ingenious about escaping. *Voila.* Alcatraz. In 1934, when Alcatraz opened as a maximum-security prison, FBI director J. Edgar Hoover predicted no prisoners would ever escape. We believe that claim to be true, but today I am going to tell you about a few inmates who tried."

The ranger led us up the steep hill past the guard towers and stopped at the top. The sun glistened on the bay, and the skyline of San Francisco jutted against the sky. At that moment Alcatraz seemed like the most beautiful place in the world.

"In 1962 the Anglin brothers and their partner, Frank Morris, succeeded in secretly building lifelike dummies for their bunks and then escaping in the middle of the night through the underground sewage pipes and into the water. Their bodies were never found. But the currents are so strong out there"—he motioned to the bay— "and the water so cold, that nobody has ever successfully escaped from Alcatraz. Not even the prisoner who snuck onto the laundry boat headed for Angel Island over there." He pointed to a small island closer to Sausalito. "The military police were waiting for him when the boat docked."

"But what about those guys you never found?" I asked, surprising myself.

"Well, the Anglin brothers and Frank Morris were very smart. They built little boats out of raincoats, just like the movie *Escape from Alcatraz* showed. But they were pretty dumb in other ways. They got thrown into Alcatraz in the first place because they robbed a bank and then returned to the same little town the next day, driving up and down Main Street."

Lemming laughed really loud, like he would have been so much smarter.

"We figure there is no way they could have survived that frigid water in the dark of night. And even if they had, they were bound to commit another crime, sooner or later, just to announce to the world that they were still alive."

Dan whispered to me, "I don't know. No bodies, no proof. Maybe those guys smartened up and went legit."

"Their escape marked the end of an era. The place was falling apart, which is why they succeeded in tunneling through the prison wall and into the sewage pipe in the first place. So Bobby Kennedy, attorney general of the United States at the time and thus head of federal prisons, closed it down shortly thereafter."

The ranger told us more stories, especially about the 1946 escape when inmates held guards hostage until the inmates themselves were taken down in a shootout. That didn't sound pretty.

When he was finished, the ranger answered any and all

questions. He seemed to like his job, and that made me like him.

After the talk we toured the main prison building, wearing headsets and listening to a tape that featured actual prisoners talking about their lives at Alcatraz and jail noises like cells clanging shut. "The cell was always part of me, even after I left," one former inmate said.

The tape also told stories about famous prisoners like Al Capone and Creepy Carpis, and of how at night inmates could hear parties at the San Francisco Yacht Club, directly across the bay. The narrator on the tape said, "Many inmates returned to prison after their release, unable to handle a new life of freedom."

What were they—crazy?

At one point the narrator instructed us to enter Cell Block G, cell No. 1. "Close your eyes and imagine what it would be like to stay in solitary confinement, with no human contact, no light, no bed, and just a hole in the floor to urinate in."

Thirty seconds of that dark silence clanging in my ears was all I could take. I would have gone nuts in "the hole," the place reserved for the very worst prisoners.

Running out of the cell, I tore off my headset and threw it on the desk near the exit. Once outside I took a deep breath, then walked over to the cliff and watched the sun set. A wide band of pink filled the sky, like cotton candy at the fair— light but almost too sweet. I stared down at the churning dark-navy waters and shivered. The ranger had told us they were filled with leopard, sand, and maybe even great white sharks. If the cold water hadn't gotten the cons, the sharks would have.

I looked below at the rocks, where the ranger said Canada geese nested in the winter. None around. They were still in Alaska, enjoying the sunlight. Mom should take note.

Back down the hill at the museum I studied the photographs on the wall. Alcatraz had first been a military fort, and later a military prison before the FBI took it over. Between 1934 and 1962 families of the guards had lived there, too. How weird it must have been to live around the most hardened criminals in the world, walking past them every morning to take the ferry to school. Then again, maybe I would have liked the excitement and danger of it. What a place to play cops and robbers!

Life magazine had done a cover story on the Alcatraz kids. They looked happy playing kickball, even with the guard tower looming in the background. Their mothers must have been basket cases, especially during an escape attempt.

In the early seventies some Indians had held a protest and camped there for several months. Didn't sound like any of them had set off bombs to make their point.

As we boarded the ferry, Dan asked where I'd gone. "I had to get outside. That cell gave me the creeps."

Dan punched my shoulder. "Luxury accommodations, huh?"

Back in San Francisco, Coach announced, "To top off this incredible day, we are headed to Pac Bell Park."

"Giants, here we come!" somebody yelled out.

I had always wanted to see Candlestick Park, the Giants' old stadium. Many players called it the worst ballpark in the National League because it was an icebox during night games and tough to hit home runs in. That's why they've built a new one. But I thought the "Stick" was kinda cool.

It bugged me that Dan had already seen the Giants play so many times. But the moment I entered the new stadium, I forgot about everything outside. I stood in awe in front of the statue of Willie Mays. I stared round and round at the thousands of seats surrounding the green grassy field with its clean, white lines.

The Giants were playing the Los Angeles Dodgers, and we managed to arrive in time for batting practice. Some of the guys ran down near the dugout and pushed and shoved through the crowd of kids, trying to get autographs. I stayed up in my seat and took it all in instead.

Sid would be jealous. Luke McHenry had made it to the big leagues, to watch a team with a history of Hall of Fame players—Mel Ott, Bill Terry, Carl Hubbell, Orlando Cepeda, Willie Mays, Juan Marichal, and Willie McCovey. Their names and uniform numbers were displayed on signboards around the park.

Hot dog Barry Bonds, the Giants' home-run hitter and left fielder, was our team's favorite, especially Lemming's. Bonds did make one great catch, jumping up against the wall in left field to get it. But no home run that night.

I preferred Jeff Kent. We were right there, cheering his

fourth grand slam of the year, which tied the Giants' season record. What a feeling that must be. You go up to bat with the bases loaded. Pow—out of the ballpark! But when Kent touched home plate, he didn't go crazy. He waved to the crowd and smiled, as if to say, "Just doing my job." I could settle for his job.

Michelle said, "Hey, if Kent were a leftie, I'll bet those boats out there in McCovey Cove would be scrambling for his home-run ball right this minute." But Kent was a right-hander and had hit it deep into left field.

In the bottom of the eighth inning, with the Giants ahead 8–1, a lot of fans started filing out. But we stayed until the very end, to ensure the victory. Even though we'd flown all night, I was too pumped to be tired and hated to leave.

On the way out, I heard a guy complain that the wind off the water made it cold, almost as cold as Candlestick. I shook my head. These people had never spent a winter in Fairbanks or a night on Alcatraz.

Chapter 14

efore the first game against Corvallis, Oregon, I searched the bleachers for Mom and Sid. After the Giants game I had called home to Fairbanks, but nobody answered. That didn't mean Mom had flown to California. She rarely answered the phone, even if she was there, unless she was expecting me or Sid to call.

I left a message. "Mom, what are you doing? I went to Alcatraz. I want to tell you about it." As if that would change her mind.

In the first inning I made a decent catch in center field for the second out. After that I relaxed. No matter what Mom decided, I had a game to play. At bat in the second inning, I walked but eventually got stranded on third.

Middle of the third inning it dawned on me. She couldn't show her face, even if she had come to the game. The FBI could be lurking anywhere, waiting to pounce, just like at the Fairbanks airport.

When we came off the field in the middle of the fifth inning, I ran to the restroom and splashed cold water on my face. The California heat was killing me. On the way back to the dugout I noticed a woman in sunglasses with curly auburn hair, standing by the fence. I shivered. Same body, same profile—Mom. I wanted to run over and shake her, tell her every gory detail about the solitary-confinement cell. But I kept walking. I could be tough, too.

Back on the bench I pretended to follow the game. I guess I didn't succeed. Dan leaned over. "What's wrong? You look like you just saw a ghost."

I tried to laugh, but nothing came out. Mom was really going to do it. It didn't matter what I said. The FBI could arrest her, right in front of the whole team. She could spend years in jail.

We made three outs, bing, bing, bing.

I shoved my hand into my glove and focused on shoving my mom out of my head. But I couldn't. Damn it. Why wouldn't she listen to me? I should have stayed in Fairbanks, threatened to give up the All Star trip, forced her hand. By leaving, I had made it too easy for her to leave, too.

In the sixth and final inning I struck out, but Michelle, Dan, and Crew scored, to tie it up, 3–3. If we could just hold off Corvallis in their last at-bat, we could win it in extra innings.

But the fourth Corvallis batter hit the ball, boom, high over the right fielder's head. By the time the relay had gotten home, the winning run had scored—4–3, Corvallis for the victory.

Afterward Coach tried to pump us up. "We're still in this tournament. We've still got a shot. Next up, Santa Rosa."

"Coach, how can we beat a team that practices twelve months a year?" Lemming asked in the dugout.

"Not with talk like that."

I looked around for Sid and Mom. Gone into thin air, just like the game.

After dinner the team headed over to the video arcade across from the motel. I stayed behind and tracked down Kathleen at the store. She confirmed that Sid and Mom had flown out but said she didn't know where they were staying.

"Yes, you do. You just don't want to tell me. I am so sick of secrets."

"Wait a minute, buster. *If* I knew where they were staying and the FBI pressured me, it would be disaster."

"You don't understand, Kathleen. We toured Alcatraz yesterday. Mom won't last in prison."

"Luke, honey, you've got to deal with this. She's not going to change her mind. After thirty-one years on the run, prison is going to be a cakewalk."

I slammed the phone down. Thanks for nothing, Kathleen. I had enough to think about with the tournament and my lousy play. Then I remembered Amy.

The phone rang before I could dig out her number. She was yelling so much, I had to hold the receiver away from my ear. Why hadn't I called, she had wanted to come to the game, what had I been doing, blah, blah, blah. Behind that angel face was a feisty woman.

At breakfast Dan tried to crack some stupid jokes, but nobody laughed. Then Lemming started talking about how he didn't like his name. "The best handle is two syllables for your first name and three syllables for your last name. All the best athletes have that."

"Right. Like Michael Jordanski, Wayne-Boy Gretskyman, Barry Bondsingdale," Crew said. A couple of guys clapped.

According to Lemming's theory, I should change my first name. To what—Tyrone, Justin, William? But I like Luke. I like my name—Luke McHenry.

Coach joined us. "Listen, team, we need to talk baseball. Any kids that play a two-month season, survive forty-below winters, and still manage to win the state championship are fighters. Go out there today and make Alaska proud."

To our amazement, we had a tied ball game, 4–4, at the top of the sixth inning. We had Santa Rosa definitely rattled, and that helped our confidence return.

Right off, Dan struck out the first two batters. But then the next guy, strutting like Barry Bonds and looking like Babe Ruth, hit his first pitch out of the park. This from a guy who hadn't done a thing the entire tournament. Our only consolation: The bases were empty.

But Dan didn't panic. Their next player sauntered to the plate and tried to stare him down. After two balls he finally took a swing and hit a pop fly to left field. I was there for the catch. We ran into the dugout, smelling bear.

"We could win this thing," I yelled.

"Yeah," said Lemming. "Let's kick their asses."

Aketachunak drew a walk and, smiling, took first base. But then Lemming struck out, and Crew hit right back to the pitcher for an easy out.

Coach put his arm around me. "Make contact again, McHenry. Just like at regionals. Your speed will carry us."

Amy's out there somewhere, I thought. She hadn't seen my great play at state. Maybe Mom and Sid, too. If we won, Mom had to stick around, and then I could convince her not to turn herself in.

Ball one. Ball two. Strike one. Ball three. Strike two. Full count. The pitch was coming. Swing? Pray for a ball? Swing and contact . . . for a lousy pop fly. I stood there, the bat heavy at my side.

Our Cinderella season was over. Just like that. Nobody made me feel bad, not even Lemming. But I hated being the one to end it all. I wanted to cry or swear or something. But I had to suck it up and shake hands with the entire lineup of smirking Santa Rosa players.

Not in ten years had a team from Fairbanks made it this far. Still, it would have been sweet to win at least one game.

As we loaded up our gear, I saw a black-haired woman and a short guy getting into a white car. I started sprinting across the parking lot, trying to catch them. All I caught was a cloud of dust.

Amy was waiting near the dugout. "Sorry you lost," she said. "You all played hard."

Coach invited Amy and her mom to join us at the pizza place on El Camino Real near our motel. The team started piling into vans, when it hit me, harder than ever. Because of me, our tournament run was ruined, blown out of the water. Why would anybody want to celebrate with me?

Amy tapped my arm. "Luke, Coach suggested you ride with us and show us the way?"

"I can't face the team. I don't want to go. Not when I screwed up big time." I threw my glove on the ground.

"Luke, you've played well for weeks. You struck out. It happens to anybody who plays the game."

"But they didn't make the last out of our whole season. No, it had to be me."

"Oh, please. It was also you who scored the winning run in the regional tournament."

I slowly picked up my glove. I wanted to dig a hole and crawl in.

"This is your chance to show you're a good sport."

A good sport, huh. Sid told me it was easy to be a good sport when you were winning, that losing showed a person's true colors.

———

Amy's mom was driving because of the busy freeway. She had taken the spinner knob off the steering wheel because only handicapped people are allowed to use one. Her mom was friendly but didn't say much. I liked how she just let Amy and me talk.

We sat at a big table and Coach ordered tons of pizza. After we had chowed down for a while and played a few video games, he stood up and cleared his throat. "It would have been nice to beat that cocky team." Looking around, he settled on me. "But you handled defeat like gentlemen. We've had a good time, haven't we?"

Everybody clapped and pounded the table.

When I got up to go to the restroom, Coach stopped me. "McHenry, you got robbed two years ago in Majors. You should have made All Stars. But sometimes life gives you a second chance, and you made the most of it."

"Thanks, Coach. It's been as great as I thought it would be. Except my last at-bat. Sorry I struck out."

"Hey, it happens to the best of us. You held your head up and that counts more than anything."

I kept watching the door, hoping that Mom or at least Sid would walk in. Then I stopped myself. She had to hide, would always be hiding if she didn't turn herself in. She wanted a second chance, too.

I realized I had to meet this family of hers. See who I looked like, see how they acted. Maybe they had even talked her out of it by now. Nothing was a done deal until she showed up at the courthouse.

The team sat around for a long time. Some guys were heading back to Alaska right away. Others were staying down longer with parents or relatives.

After I left Fairbanks, Mom had talked to Amy's parents and okayed my staying with them for a few days. I wondered how comfortable I was going to feel at their house—especially when they found out about Mom. But I wasn't ready to return to Fairbanks either. I had an open-return ticket. Maybe I'd just stay until they kicked me out.

The whole team went back to the motel to check out. "I didn't know you and Amy were such good friends," Dan said, as we packed up our room.

What was I supposed to say? "We're not. Actually, I'm staying, Dan, because my mom's going to jail."

I grabbed the baseball cap off his head instead. "Didn't you know—we're getting hitched tomorrow? Amy wants to marry a younger man so that she doesn't outlive her husband. Want to stick around and be my best man?"

He wrestled his cap away from me, then zipped up his bag. He was staying with his cousins in Santa Cruz for a week. Hopefully he wouldn't be reading any newspapers.

Later I called Kathleen collect when Amy's mom stopped for gas. "I want to see Mom one last time."

"You could go to her arraignment day after tomorrow, ten A.M., at the Alameda County courthouse in downtown Berkeley."

"I don't feel so good, Kathleen. We lost both our games in

the tournament, the last one because of me. I popped out."

"That's too bad, Luke. I know how much this tournament meant to you. But you have played so well all summer. Don't blame yourself for one little mistake."

"But now it's all over."

"I hope you've had some fun."

"Yeah."

"Listen, Sid knows where you're staying. I'm sure he'll call you."

"I don't know what to do."

"Talk to Amy. You can trust her."

Amy's house was ranch style, all the rooms on one level. A great layout for a wheelchair, with ramps at the front and back doors. Unpacked boxes were stacked against the walls in some of the rooms, but the place still seemed organized. The living room had these big white leather couches, almost too nice to sit on.

The guest room had its own bathroom, with samples of shampoo and conditioner in a little basket and matching monogrammed towels. If Mom ever even thought about buying towels like that, what initials would she use?

I was still standing in the bathroom when Amy called through the bedroom door and suggested we take a ride. We hadn't gotten one block from her house before I started in on Mom's whole story.

When Amy didn't react I figured she already knew.

"No way. I only worked at the store for a month. But it

didn't take a rocket scientist to notice something was seriously dragging her down."

"You're not shocked at what she did?"

"Luke, it was years ago, during a war that divided our country. How can I judge? It doesn't sound like they meant for somebody to die." Amy was amazing. Here we were, driving on this busy street in a new place, and she wasn't rattled at all that my mom was a criminal.

"Then why is she turning herself in?" I asked.

"Because it was wrong and I guess if she doesn't serve some time, she'll never get over her guilt. I don't know. It can't have been an easy decision." She turned and looked at me. "Why do you expect *me* to know everything?"

"Because you're brilliant." She couldn't help but laugh. "I don't know. I just don't know anything right now. Am I supposed to go to her arraignment? I don't want to see her arrested, but I might not see her again for a long time."

"I bet she doesn't expect you there." Amy looked at me, then quickly back at the road. "What is your gut telling you? That's my guide, seeing as my brain gets too fried and my legs aren't much use."

"Your gut's pretty small."

"Shut up."

We drove around Concord, the suburb twenty miles from Berkeley where Amy's family lived. I wasn't paying much attention to the scenery and had no idea where we were.

"I need to talk to Sid," I announced after minutes of silence.

"Let's go home, then, and see if he's called. Maybe my mom knows where he's staying."

"How are your parents going to feel about what my mom did?"

"Hey, after my accident, nothing will ever seem earth-shattering again."

"But my mom caused a death. She's not the victim like you were."

"Luke, get out of the car. How many times have I told you not to call me a victim?" Amy pulled over to the curb and waited.

I just sat there. What did she expect me to do? Start walking the streets of this strange town, begging for my dinner and a place to sleep? What had my mom been thinking, setting me up to stay with somebody I barely knew? Amy couldn't make me get out. I would just sleep in the van if I had to and catch the next plane home tomorrow.

We sat there in silence for several minutes. "I'm sorry, Luke. I shouldn't have yelled at you. I hate being called a victim. It sounds like I have no control over my life."

I felt like I was going to cry, like I was eight years old and didn't get invited to my best friend's birthday party. First the strikeout, now this. I couldn't seem to do anything right that day.

I was breathing hard, gripping the sides of the bucket seat. I had to pull it together. Like it or not, I was stuck down here in California.

I took another breath and tried again. "I didn't mean to call you that, Amy. I could never do what you've done, living your life as if nothing had happened. You're so tough. I wish I was."

"You will be when the time comes."

When we got home, Amy's mom opened the door to the garage and waved me in. "Your stepfather's on the phone."

"Sid, I've got to talk to Mom."

"She wants to see you, too."

Chapter 16

I stood in the middle of Oakland's Jack London Square and searched for my mother. Amy sat by the water fountain, sketching in her notebook. Every now and then I would glance over at her. One time she waved. But no sign of Mom.

Finally, a woman in a big sun hat and yellow high-heeled sandals walked by and stopped by a trash can a few feet away. I went and threw away my soda can, then followed her across the square. How weird to be chasing your own mother in a strange city in California.

"Thank you for coming. It means so much to see you," she said, her voice low.

We started walking together.

I tried to stay cool. "You look funky. Not your usual understated self." She smiled.

"How did your parents treat you?" I asked. "I'd like to have been a fly on the wall for that meeting."

"I wish you could have been there. They want to meet you."

She looked at me. "Are you terribly disappointed? You played so well in the tournament, but I know your last at-bat must have upset you."

"Yeah. I panicked, got nervous, and swung too soon. A stupid mistake. I really wanted us to win. I don't know. I'm trying to remember that we had a great season. I'm just bummed it's over. It went by so fast."

She nodded. "I'm very proud of you."

It wasn't until then that I noticed the pin on her sweater, the one I had made in Cub Scouts. My third-grade school picture was mounted inside a frame made of braided yellow and blue plastic cord, the kind you make key chains out of at camp. I'm wearing the goofiest smile, and my hair is slicked down like it had ten pounds of grease on it. I remember thinking I was so cool back then. Maybe that's how Mom saw me still, a nerdy little kid who knew nothing about the real world.

I stayed in Cub Scouts only a year. Mom didn't even want me to join up. But Dan's dad was the cubmaster, and he encouraged me to come.

"They probably feel sorry for Luke because he doesn't have a father," I overheard Mom tell Kathleen one night after I'd first joined.

"Shush, Faith. It's good for him."

"No, it isn't. The Boy Scouts are militaristic and narrow-minded."

"I am going to miss you so much, Luke."

I touched her arm. "Mom, I went on a tour of Alcatraz. Prison is awful. Have you thought of that?"

"Nothing could be worse than this guilt."

We stopped in front of the statue of Jack London. "My language arts teacher said that for all his adventures and success, Jack London still got depressed."

"Yes," Mom said, daring to squeeze my hand. "So depressed that he killed himself. Imagine writing *The Call of the Wild* and not being satisfied. I've got to do better than that."

"Mom, I can't face going to the courthouse tomorrow."

"I understand. I wish it was behind me."

That night Amy and I went over to a pond near her house. On the path in the park some lady buzzed by us on a motorized wheelchair. "Ever think of getting one of those?"

She shook her head. "Too cumbersome. Can't you just see me trying to maneuver down a high school hallway in one of those? Talk about a traffic jam. This manual one is much easier to turn."

We stopped at a bench in front of the pond. "I don't know if I can sit in that courtroom and watch them arrest my mom."

"There are other ways to show your support." Amy threw some bread crumbs out on the water. "I thought you already told her you weren't coming."

"But I don't want the judge and everybody to think I hate her."

"My, aren't we full of ourselves. Do you really think you have that much influence on the situation? Stop worrying, Luke. I think it's a done deal." Her voice got louder. "I'm so sick of people who think they are the only ones with problems."

"I didn't mean—"

"Forget it. I'm just feeling sorry for myself today." This wasn't the Amy I knew. One more thing I didn't have a clue about. One more time I put my foot in my mouth. I decided to try a lighter subject.

"Geez, these ducks are huge. I guess we're not the only ones feeding them," I said, trying to laugh. "I think I read somewhere that we're supposed to be feeding them something healthier than moldy bread. But I can't remember what."

"This bread is perfectly fine. It's not moldy."

Another bomb-out. Silently we watched a flock of ducks scarf up the food.

"I don't think I can handle it, okay? But I can't miss out on Mom's biggest deal, either."

"I would say the bombing thirty-one years ago was a whole lot worse for your mother than tomorrow will be. I think she'll be relieved, like a big weight has been lifted from her shoulders."

"What do you know?" I grabbed the bag from Amy's hand and threw out more bread.

"Nothing, I guess. At least not the easy answer you want. Even on my worst days in this wheelchair"—her voice started to shake— "I'm still glad that I'm alive, that I didn't die in the accident. I'm not sure I should say this, but maybe your mother wonders why she lived when that kid died because of her mistake."

Long after we ran out of bread, we continued to sit and watch the ducks.

On the way back to her house I looked at my watch—eight o'clock. "Do you think the mall is still open?"

"Probably until nine in the summertime. Why?"

"Will you drive me over there so I can buy some decent clothes to wear to court tomorrow?"

She nodded, her brown eyes bright.

"Come with me tomorrow, Amy. We can sneak in and listen from the back of the courtroom."

She laughed. "Hey, if you want to go incognito, rolling into the courtroom with me won't do it." She sped up. "Sid will be there. And I'll be waiting when it's over."

The next morning I stood outside the police and fire department, right next door to the Berkeley courthouse, and waited again. I had on my new black dress shirt and khaki pants that Amy had helped me pick out. The courthouse was an awful green-blue color. I thought courthouses were supposed to be fancy-looking. Not this one. It was the ugliest building I'd ever seen.

I paced back and forth, holding the doughnut I couldn't

seem to eat. When I saw a beggar sitting on the curb, I handed it to him. He grinned, revealing jagged, yellow teeth. "Thank you, son."

I walked away without smiling back. What if they had gone in another entrance? I could have missed the whole thing. Maybe that was what I wanted.

At about nine forty-five A.M., two women, one older, one younger, walked arm in arm with Mom up the sidewalk from the opposite direction. I ducked behind a Dumpster before they could see me. Mom was wearing a light blue suit I'd never seen before.

Sid followed behind with two men. One man was old, skinny, and gray. But then I noticed how straight and tall he stood. No stooped shoulders or beer belly on this guy. He must be my grandfather. The younger guy looked like him, but was taller and more muscular. He must be one of Mom's brothers. Did I look like them? I wondered, wishing I had a mirror just then.

They stopped in front of the courthouse and a dark-haired woman in a gray business suit came out the front door. Mom hugged her and the woman shook hands with everyone else. Then they stepped inside. That must be her lawyer. I'd expected her lawyer to be more of an aging hippie type that had also been against the Vietnam War. I ran into the building, hoping to stay close to them, but not wanting them to see me. When they stopped in front of the elevator, I ducked in the stairwell and sprinted up the stairs, two at a time.

I was still panting when the elevator arrived on the second floor. People crowded the corridor, but no one seemed to notice Mom's group. I felt like I was swimming underwater, with not enough breath to reach the surface. How come Mom hadn't already drowned?

They stopped in front of a double wooden door with an engraved brass sign—DEPARTMENT 202. Without hesitating, Sid opened one of the doors and they all filed into the nearly empty courtroom and sat in the third row. I stood in back, in the far right corner, near the exit. After they were seated, Sid turned around and raised his eyebrows at me. Leave it to Sid to know that I was there.

The judge, about Mom's age but wearing lots more makeup, entered almost immediately. "All rise. Judge Martha Simpson's court is now in session."

Yes, this judge would understand. She had lived through the Vietnam War, too.

Mom stood straight and tall beside her attorney. But my legs almost bottomed out when the clerk read, "The People of the state of California vs. Mary Margaret Cunningham, court case number 9540."

"Counsel, are you ready?" Both attorneys nodded. Mom's attorney touched her hand and Mom turned toward her for just a second.

The judge then sat down and motioned for us to do the same. I inched into the back row. But I really wanted to bolt.

Mom remained standing. What was her real hair color

now? Still dark brown like her sister's? Or gray like her mom's?

In row three Mom's parents sat stone still. I wondered what it had been like for them to read about their daughter's crime in the newspaper. Or had the FBI shown up at their door first?

The clerk began reading. "Mary Margaret Cunningham, you are hereby charged with a first-degree felony for the use of explosives; and second-degree murder for the reckless endangerment of life during the bombing of the ROTC offices in Harmon Gym at the University of California Berkeley on June 1, 1970, during which Stephen Dolan died."

Murder two? That couldn't be right. My throat tightened up and I felt like I couldn't breathe. If she was charged with murder, she'd be in jail forever.

"Your Honor, the state moves to amend these charges."

"Proceed," the judge said.

The other lawyer, a tough-looking guy in a black suit, walked up to the judge's bench and handed her some documents. "These reflect the discussion Counsel Winston and I held with you ten days ago."

The judge nodded, but still took time to read through the papers. Not a sound could be heard in the courtroom. Nothing. It was freaky, like the world had suddenly stopped.

Finally the judge looked at the two attorneys and sighed. "Yes, I did reluctantly agree to this plea bargain and the waiving of the pre-sentencing hearing."

She then looked sternly at Mom. "Mary Margaret Cunningham, the state of California now charges you with"—the judge hesitated—"involuntary manslaughter, for the bombing of the ROTC offices at the University of California Berkeley on June 1, 1970. How do you plead?"

"Guilty, Your Honor."

Guilty. My body jerked and my head hit the back of the bench with a thud.

What a story for the media: "Son Knocks Himself Out Because of Mother's Fugitive Past."

"Ms. Cunningham," the judge intoned, "you will be sequestered in the Alameda County Jail at the Santa Rita facility. Due to the unusual circumstances in this case, I have agreed to hold the sentencing as soon as possible. Therefore, it will take place this Friday at nine A.M. All concerned parties are invited to give statements at that time."

Mom's attorney stood up. "Your Honor, based on Ms. Cunningham's exemplary community service and work history in Fairbanks, Alaska, I request that bail be set."

The judge frowned. "Counselor, is it not true that this woman has been a fugitive from the law since the crime was committed?" Mom would have been better off with an old geezer judge.

"Yes, Your Honor. But Ms. Cunningham is now determined to pay for her crime, even though it means leaving her son and husband."

"Thirty-one years as a fugitive strongly suggests the possibility that Ms. Cunningham could be a flight risk. Request for bail denied." Mom's shoulders sagged as the judge pounded the gavel.

They were treating her like a criminal. She didn't mean to do it, I wanted to yell out. But I clenched my jaws shut. She had done it and just pleaded guilty.

The guard walked over to Mom. But before she turned to face him, Mom scanned the courtroom, her eyes like those of a moose calf that was trapped on Farewell Avenue in Fairbanks last winter. Cars had honked and people had jumped out to stare at the calf's mother bleeding to death in the road.

Mom had stopped me from getting out of the car. "Hopefully that little one will survive," she had said then, turning up a side street and taking the long way home.

I started up the courtroom aisle.

Mom looked at me, her eyes watery behind her lenses. Glasses. She wore glasses now and no makeup. She had turned back into Mary Margaret Cunningham. No more contacts. No more Faith McHenry.

She mouthed the words, "I love you." Her eyes were clear and smooth now, like pebbles in a stream.

Then, as if a steel rod had suddenly been shoved up her spine, Mom pulled back her shoulders and held out her wrists for the guard to put on the handcuffs.

I remembered what Kathleen had told me the day I left Fairbanks. "Ice water runs through your mother's veins. How else has she survived all these years on the run?"

Or was it something Michelle had said about baseball?

Whatever, I hoped Mom had it, and not the warm slush moving through my body.

She never looked back. Not even when the guard opened the side door and photographers and reporters waited on the other side.

Chapter 16

A photographer shoved his camera in my face, and I ran out the courtroom door before Sid could stop me. But I froze on the shiny hardwood floor—until I spotted the GENTLEMEN door and sprinted into a stall.

Sid's voice followed me. "Luke, you can come out. Nobody's in here."

I looked under the door and saw only his feet on the marbled floor. "How did the media find out?" I asked, emerging from the stall.

Sid shook his head. "Let's get out of here."

"Sid, they took her to jail. We've got to do something."

"Luke, she's turned herself in. It's all over. All the waiting is finally over."

"You sound like you've given up."

Sid shook his head. "It was her decision."

"Nobody told me there was going to be a sentencing too."

"You haven't been easy to talk to about this. All you wanted to do was convince your mother not to turn herself in."

"I came today."

Sid put his arm around me. "Yes, you did, and I can only imagine how much that meant to her."

Another man walked into the restroom. I started back into the stall until his words stopped me. "Luke, I'm your uncle Mark."

I stared at his brown, receding hairline and expensive suit. I couldn't hug this guy or even seem to shake his hand. I just stood there, nodding like a goon. "Did you know about me?"

"Sadly, no. We didn't even know your mother was alive until a week ago. But when we got together, all she could talk about was you." He took my elbow. "The rest of the family is across the hall in the conference room. Why don't you come meet them?"

"Luke, my grandson," the older woman said. A month ago I hadn't even known I had a grandmother. "We're all so anxious to get to know you."

Getting up and giving me a hug, she resembled an older, more stylish Mom. I stared around the room. I didn't look like any of them.

"Luke, I'm your aunt Carol. I'm glad you decided to come today." This woman looked like Mom, too, but prettier except for her frown. I knew I needed to say something, but my mouth wouldn't move. Not even when Uncle Mark asked me about the baseball tournament.

"You have other uncles and aunts and many cousins up in Spokane and Seattle. Unfortunately they all couldn't come down, but they all want to meet you. We hope you'll come to visit soon," my grandmother said softly.

I didn't fit in with these people. I couldn't handle meeting even more of them.

Stupidly I blurted out, "I have a friend waiting for me. I have to go."

Mark put his hand on my arm. "Luke—"

"Was Mom wild as a kid?" I asked.

He shook his head. "Not at all."

"So how come— Never mind."

"We never figured that out, Luke," the older man said, shaking my hand. "I'm your grandfather."

I looked around for Sid. "So can just anybody who wants to, speak at Mom's sentencing? People could get up and say horrible things about her."

"Within reason," Mom's attorney said. "Hello, Luke. I'm Diane Winston." She extended her hand, then turned to the others and said, "Thanks for coming today, everyone. I know that Mary Margaret appreciated all the support. We've survived the first hurdle. But I have to warn you that the media will be lurking, trying to talk to anybody who ever knew Mary Margaret."

"How did all those reporters find out?" Sid asked. "I thought the negotiations were confidential."

"I'd imagine the prosecuting attorney or the Dolan family alerted them. This has remained a high-profile case all these years."

"Were those the Dolans sitting in the front row?" Carol asked.

"Yes," Diane said. "Mrs. Dolan and her daughter. Mr. Dolan died about ten years ago."

"Diane, can we check on Mary Margaret later today?" my grandmother asked. "It's her birthday, you know. We already had her presents and cake last night at the hotel." She stopped and coughed into a linen handkerchief. "I have no idea why she picked today of all days . . ."

"No, her birthday's in October," I said, perspiration starting to trickle down the sides of my face. I'd never sweated like this before, not even during All Stars.

Sid put his arm around me. "You're right, Luke. We always celebrated your mom's birthday in October."

Won't we still? I wondered.

"I have Amy's phone number, so I'll call you later. But here's mine, just in case." He handed me the phone number of his motel. "Maybe we can all have dinner together."

When I arrived at the coffee shop, I found Amy waiting, as promised. "So how did it go?"

"Okay." I sat down at her table.

"Okay? How did your mom do? What's her family like?"

"What's with all the questions?" The waitress came and I ordered two hot dogs.

"I don't look like any of Mom's family," I said, playing with a napkin. "There were lots of reporters around."

Across from us a kid in a booth was looking at us. I felt like telling him to bug off. Instead I stared back until he looked away. Then I stood up and told Amy I wanted to leave.

"You're not used to people staring at you, are you?" she whispered, motioning me to sit back down. "It drives my cousin so crazy that she won't go out in public with me."

"Doesn't it bother you?" I asked, after the boy left with his friends.

"At first it did. But I've finally learned that if people can't get past my wheelchair it's their problem and there's nothing I can do about it."

"But how can you stand it?"

"Luke, I don't have any other choice except to hide at home. This wheelchair makes me stick out, makes me different."

The waitress brought my order and I slathered mustard on the dogs. "There were tons of photographers, and now Mom's picture is probably going to be plastered across the newspapers. Maybe even mine and everybody in the world's going to know and—"

"And you're going to feel stupid because people might stare at you. It's not your fault but you still have to deal with it."

"Great." I took a couple of bites, then looked up. "The judge is still going to sentence her on Friday, even though the plea bargain has already been set. People can give comments if they want."

"The victim's family has a right to be heard."

"They were there today. They must be out for blood."

"No, they lost a son."

"I thought you were on Mom's side."

"You don't have a clue, Luke. This isn't about taking sides. It's about loss and trying to move on." Amy played with her gold locket, her dark eyes staring into space.

"But my mom didn't mean to do it. She's going to jail. Isn't that enough? Besides, none of this will bring him back."

"The college kid who hit me didn't mean to do it either." Amy placed both hands on the table. "Yet winning a big insurance settlement and knowing he was serving time in jail still didn't erase my anger."

"What did?"

"Meeting with the driver and letting him apologize in person. He had written me a letter, but meeting face to face had more of an impact."

"What? You actually sat down and talked to the scum?"

"Grow up, Luke. He made a mistake, a huge mistake. So did your mom."

I finished my hot dogs in silence.

"I didn't mean to get heavy, Luke. Why don't we check out U.C. Berkeley? My meter's good for another hour."

When I didn't answer, she nudged me. "Come on. Let's

look around the Berkeley campus. It's just a few blocks from here."

I hesitated. Why would I want to visit the place where Stephen Dolan died?

"This is where the sixties happened, man." Amy clicked her fingers and tried to look groovy. "All that revolutionary activity started right here."

She began rolling out of the restaurant and I had no choice but to follow. I paid the cashier and ran to catch up with her.

As we walked around, I wondered where Mom had hung out. But when we passed by People's Park on Dwight Way and Telegraph Avenue and read the plaque, I knew.

IN MAY 1969 STUDENTS TOOK OVER THIS LAND
TO FORM THE PEOPLE'S PARK. HUNDREDS OF
PROTESTS TOOK PLACE HERE UNTIL 1975 WHEN
THE WAR IN VIETNAM FINALLY ENDED.

I imagined Mom marching around carrying a big sign, "HELL NO, WE WON'T GO!"

I remembered the old photographs I'd seen: tear-gas bombs thrown into a crowd of college kids, cop cars over-turned, National Guardsmen arresting students. What a crazy time. Mom was part of it. In a weird way, so was I.

I didn't see any sign saying where the ROTC office was located and sure didn't feel like asking anybody. It probably wasn't even in the same place anymore. Maybe they even moved it after the bombing.

We eventually ended up on the famous Telegraph Avenue, where street vendors, musicians, and panhandlers hung out just like Dan had described. It looked like the hippies were still alive and well.

Walking back to the car, I wondered if my father had also protested against the war. I knew so little about him.

The afternoon sun had broken through the fog, so Amy put down all the car windows. Mom goes to jail and I'm driving around with all the freedom in the world. So why didn't I feel free? My head throbbed like somebody had put a clamp on my brain and screwed it up tight.

That night my head still hurt, so I turned down Sid's invitation to go out to eat. Instead I watched some television with Amy and then lay in bed for hours before I fell asleep.

But by six o'clock the next morning I had already collected the *San Francisco Chronicle* from Amy's front porch. My hands shook as I pulled the rubber band off the newspaper. It wasn't like I didn't know what had happened. But reading about it in the paper—then the world would know, too, and I couldn't hide anymore.

At first I just stood there, holding it. Finally I whipped the paper open, hoping not to find anything. No such luck. Front-page center—Mom, with her lips in a frozen half smile, and handcuffs on her wrists.

I almost lost last night's enchiladas right there on the porch steps. Mom never wanted her picture taken, not even at Christmas. Here it was on the wire service worldwide.

RADICAL FUGITIVE
FINALLY CONFESSES

In Berkeley, California, yesterday Mary Margaret Cunningham, alias Faith McHenry, turned herself in to law enforcement authorities for the second-degree murder of Stephen Dolan. Dolan was killed in the bombing of the University of California Berkeley's ROTC offices on June 1, 1970. A fugitive from the law for thirty-one years, Cunningham has lived with her son and husband in Fairbanks, Alaska. . . .

I could just hear the debates at kitchen tables around the country. "It's about time. Those radicals had no respect for what our boys were going through over in that jungle."

"Hey, we're talking about Vietnam. Without those protests we'd still be involved in that idiotic war."

I looked at her photo again, then flipped through the rest of the paper. On the back page of the main section was a reproduction of the FBI Most Wanted poster. Mom had sad eyes, even then.

There were no photos of me.

Chapter 17

Amy's parents weren't around at breakfast, so I shoved the paper over to her. She scanned the front page, then whistled. "I expected coverage, but not this."

I stared at the photo again. Mom wanted the Dolans to forgive her. And that wasn't going to happen in a cold courtroom during the sentencing.

I looked at Amy. "It's not over, is it? Mom going to jail doesn't make it all go away."

She shook her head. "Nope."

I poured myself some cereal. "Yesterday you said that meeting with the guy who hit you really helped. But how could you stand to face him?"

"It wasn't easy, but it was so much better than feeling sorry for myself. They call it restorative justice, and when my mom heard about it she begged Dad and me to do it because neither of us would talk about how angry we were. I had been trying to pretend it had never happened. But of course that was a little hard when I was reminded of it every minute of my life." She looked down at her wheelchair.

"What we actually had was a survivor-offender meeting. They also have victim-offender mediations when it's a crime like robbery and the offender can make restitution. But there was no way Tom could give me back my legs." She rolled over to the refrigerator to get some orange juice.

"After our meeting, Tom wrote us from jail every so often. When he got out, he finished college and then went into the Peace Corps in Africa. He still sends us Christmas cards. Every letter mentions how grateful he is that we forgave him."

"It does sound like he turned his life around."

Amy's experience reminded me of the television show earlier this summer that had featured something similar. It was pretty amazing how the people forgave the criminals.

Would something like that be possible with Mom and the Dolans? I wondered. I tried to picture Mrs. Dolan in the courtroom, but I hadn't wanted to look in her face, so I had no idea whether she seemed forgiving or not. I sat there cracking my knuckles.

Amy grimaced at me. "Must you?"

"Sorry. I guess I do it when I'm nervous."

"But you didn't do it the night we went to Skipper's." She smiled. "I guess we were having too much fun."

"Could a meeting like that help my mom?" Amy nodded. "But what if it just makes her feel worse?"

"I would think that the person who committed the crime would need it even more than the victim. Tom sure did."

"Do you think the Dolans would agree to a meeting?"

"It's worth a try."

"So who would set it up?"

"I'm not sure but my mom would know. I just heard her car pull in."

"Your parents probably won't want me to stay here any longer when they see this." I pointed to the paper.

"They already know."

"And they're not upset?"

"My dad, the dedicated Army guy, probably would have been upset before my accident. But now we know that everybody suffers in a tragedy, no matter who caused it. Besides, you didn't do it, Luke."

So why did I feel so lousy?

"Actually, they're glad you're staying here. They feel guilty enough moving me yet another time."

"Thanks, Amy, for everything." I got up and put my cereal bowl in the sink. I looked over at her reading the paper. Now that we were friends and I felt comfortable around her, I'd almost forgotten how pretty she was and how intimidated I'd been when I first met her.

Amy's mother suggested that I talk to Sid first and then Mom's lawyer. "A meeting can take place anytime, not necessarily right now," she explained.

I called Sid at his motel. "How are you doing this morning, Luke?"

"Okay until I saw the paper. Did you go see Mom at the jail?"

"No, it seems that visiting hours are limited to Wednesday evenings and Saturdays."

"Man. So you're going tonight then?"

"Yes. I did talk to her, though. She seems to be holding up and said to be sure and tell you thanks for coming yesterday."

"I feel so stupid just running out on those relatives. Did they expect me for dinner last night?"

"Don't worry. I didn't go either. I think we all needed to sort things out. Give it time. You'll get used to them."

"Have *you?*" I finally got him to laugh, sort of. "Do you think jail time will finally help Mom get over this?"

"God, I hope so." He sounded really tired.

"Sid." I cleared my throat. "I need to talk to you and Diane about something."

"That probably would be a good idea. You never got to sit down with her the way your mom and I did." Just like Sid, he didn't ask what I wanted to discuss. He took my word that it was important. "I'll call Diane and see if she can meet with us in the next day or two."

"It's about the sentencing. Is there any way she could see us today?"

Diane squeezed us in at three o'clock that afternoon. She worked in one of those fancy law firms with the huge wooden doors and modern furniture. Mom must be paying her a fortune, but where was the money coming from? Her dad?

Diane directed us into her office and offered us something to drink. I shook my head. I wanted to get this over with.

Diane wasn't surprised at my idea. Sid raised his eyebrows but listened.

"I've been thinking about it too, Luke," Diane said. "Why don't we bring it up with your mother later, after the sentencing, when emotions aren't so high?"

"But that's the whole point. The sentencing is going to be another public humiliation and won't accomplish what Mom needs. Maybe a meeting with the Dolans could even take the place of the sentencing. I mean her sentence has already been decided, right? Why go through the motions?"

"I wish that were the case, Luke, but your mother is required by law to appear for sentencing, even though it's already been agreed upon."

"Okay. Then let's do it before. Then the sentencing will be much easier on everybody."

"It is a fine idea. But your mother has to want it and—"

"I can convince her, and you can set it up."

"Whoa. Hold on here." Diane backed up her chair and stood up. "Even if your mother agrees to a meeting, the Dolans have to sign on, too."

"Wouldn't they want to hear her apology in a more private setting?"

"I don't know. Perhaps. Hopefully. But it could be something they're not up to doing yet, nor your mom." Diane looked at me. "A face-to-face meeting could be even more difficult. The Dolans could grill her pretty hard."

"My mom is a lot stronger than you think. This could help her get over her guilt."

"Nobody has to tell me how strong Mary Margaret is."

"Luke," Sid said, his cool voice cutting through the stuffy room. "Diane has been very supportive throughout this whole thing. It's your mother's decision and she may not be ready for it yet."

"Let me talk to her about it."

"Fine," Diane said, sighing, "but it's highly unlikely the judge would approve of such a meeting until after the sentencing. And your mother doesn't need this distraction right now, so why don't you just wait until next week?"

"No, now. I might be back in Alaska. Who's calling the shots here, Sid?"

"Your mother is. She always has." Sid sounded like he'd given up.

"Then let *her* decide, please, Sid," I said.

"Luke has been left out of all the decisions until now, Diane. Faith would want to at least hear about this."

Sid turned to me. "The thing is, on the phone last night your mother asked that you not come to see her at this jail. She wants you to wait until she's settled at her permanent placement where there'll be a regular visiting room. At the Santa Rita jail you'd have to talk to her through a—"

"Sid, I can handle it and I'm going to persuade her, you'll see. And when she agrees, what's the next step, Diane?"

"I'll talk to the prosecuting attorney and get the ball rolling. But first, Mary Margaret has got to want to do it."

"She will," I said.

"And we mustn't forget the Dolans. In fact, maybe we should check with them first." Diane tapped her pen on the desk. "No, let's wait and see what your mother says. Good luck, Luke." She walked over and shook my hand.

"Tonight it is. Saturday will be too late."

Chapter 18

It felt good that somebody finally listened to my opinion—until Sid and I went to get something to eat and he tried to talk me out of it. "I think you might want to see your mom first, make sure she's doing all right before you spring this on her."

"Wait a minute. You backed me up at Diane's office. Why are you changing your mind now?"

"That came out wrong. See how she's doing and if it feels right, go ahead. It's just that she's only been in this place a little more than twenty-four hours."

The Santa Rita jail was about thirteen miles from Berkeley, so we took the 580 freeway and had to drive a long way through bumper-to-bumper traffic. Sid had wanted to get there plenty early to make sure we both got signed up for visiting slots. We ended up sitting in the parking lot of the jail for half an hour, just doing nothing.

You couldn't tell it was a prison from the outside—no high fences or barbed wire. The place was huge, with several sprawling buildings. Somebody had told Sid that it had 3,300 inmates and was the largest county jail in the country. Wonderful. Mom just loved crowds.

It was sweltering in the car, so we both got out and looked around, stopping at the antique clock in front of the jail. It actually worked: five forty P.M. The marker said it had originally stood on the corner of Third and Market Streets in San Francisco, where it had survived the 1906 earthquake. How come this jail got it? I wondered. Surely the prisoners weren't considered honored citizens.

As we were reading the sign, a guard walked up and told us about the no loitering rule. "You'll have to wait in the car. Sorry, folks. We can't be too careful."

Sid asked if we could wait in the lobby. "Afraid not. The lobby is just for attorneys."

Great. What if we had walked, taken the bus, or biked? I felt like asking the guy, but I didn't want to be insulted further.

Sid synchronized his watch with the antique clock. But it turned out that it was fast by a minute or two, so we still had to wait when we got to the front door. Fortunately the guard wasn't around. By now other people had gathered. They didn't look seedy like I had expected. Just normal people— some kids, maybe a couple of girlfriends or wives.

Did I look seedy? My mom was in jail.

Right on the dot of six o'clock another guard opened the

front door and let us walk into the lobby, where we were met by glorious cool air. At least they had air conditioning for the prisoners or maybe just in the lobby for show.

At the front desk Sid signed us up for visitor passes. He had to fill out this long form: name, address, date of birth, driver's license number, inmate name, housing location, and PFN, whatever that was. Since we didn't know, we had to go ask the clerk at the information table. It turned out Mom was in the maximum-security unit for females, thanks to the judge who wouldn't give her bail. She was in with all the really bad criminals.

At the bottom of the form Sid listed my name where it asked for "others in vehicle." Since kids under eighteen had to be with a parent or guardian to visit an inmate, they wanted proof that Sid was my guardian.

Sid went up to the desk and tried to explain to the clerk that Mom was my parent. But the woman wasn't going to let me go in until Sid pitched a fit, which he never does, and insisted on seeing the supervisor. Actually he used a very quiet but firm voice that radiated *Don't mess with me. I am a bulldog who will not give up.*

Finally some guy in a uniform came out and listened to Sid. "Sir, this young man has traveled all the way from Alaska to see his mother. I know that your facility supports family relations. Isn't there some way we can resolve this?"

Right then I'd have traded a month in Siberia for this freeze out.

Sergeant Lopez said he had to check with the watch commander. More waiting. Finally he came back out and agreed to let me visit this one time if I had proof that I was Mom's son. I felt like saying "go look at her and then come back and compare us." But then I don't really look like Mom.

The other visitors were looking at us. I dug through my wallet and found my medical insurance card with mom's name on it. I also showed him my Chena Middle School photo ID. I now looked so much older I didn't think he would recognize me, but he did.

Before Sergeant Lopez left he said to Sid, "I'd suggest you be named this kid's official guardian as soon as possible. It sounds like his mother's going to be in jail a while."

Thanks, buddy. I felt like knocking him down. Did he enjoy making us look like fools?

When that was finally settled, the clerk handed us both a list of rules to read and sign. The list went on forever:

No contraband—bringing in drugs, alcohol, firearms, or explosives is a crime and the visitor could be arrested. Like duh. I would want to get my mom into any more trouble.

Visitors aren't allowed to have cameras. Who in their right mind would want to take a photo in this place?

No cell phones, purses, backpacks, etc. No smoking, food, or drink. Man, I felt like I was the one in prison. The red tape was driving me crazy. It's like they did everything they could to keep you out. I guess that was the point. Less trouble for them.

The kicker was that after all this trouble I would get only twenty minutes with my mom. First the clerk said that Sid and I would have to split the time, since I was a minor under eighteen and had to be with Sid the entire time. She looked at Sid and said, "And you can't visit a prisoner more than once during a visiting session."

"Let me see Sergeant Lopez again."

This time he quickly agreed to let us have two periods. Then he looked at me and pointed at Sid. "He'll have to wait in the room while you're visiting, though." I nodded. Did he want to put me in handcuffs, too?

Then, after all this, the clerk told us we'd have to wait outside and come back at exactly six thirty P.M. Sid's face was so red I thought he was going to blow a gasket. I was just breathing heavy.

By the time we walked to the car and back, it would be time. Mom must have been going nuts with all these stupid rules. If this was how they treated visitors, what did they do to the inmates?

Back at the front door at exactly six thirty P.M., Sid and I showed our passes and IDs to the guard, then were ushered through a metal detector, similar to one at an airport. With everything else going wrong, I expected it to start beeping.

On the other side, we walked through these big metal gates, which clanged behind us. This was it. No turning back. My hands felt clammy.

Guards with huge key rings hanging from their belts stood around under huge fluorescent lights. A couple were shouting orders. Around here nobody did anything softly. Mom was probably freaking out. She liked quiet. Said she'd gotten used to it, all those years living alone. My ears were already ringing.

A guard walked over, studied our passes, and pointed to one of three big control booths. There the watch commander for Mom's unit took our passes and then pushed a button. Soon a vehicle like a golf cart pulled up and yet another guard appeared and motioned for us to climb aboard. "This will take you directly to the visiting area."

I must have looked shocked. "Pretty nifty, isn't it? It runs by sensors and takes you only where it's programmed to go. This place is so big that everybody gets around this way and it sure saves on security costs. The prisoners can be handcuffed to this." He pointed to a railing attached to the cart.

We scooted down the hallway. I felt like I was in some sci-fi movie and tried to enjoy the only decent part of this nightmare. Sid and I looked at each other a couple of times but didn't speak.

The vehicle stopped at a door marked VISITING AREA C. Sid touched my shoulder as we disembarked. Maybe he thought he had to buck me up. It wasn't far from the truth. I felt about an inch from freaking out myself. When the guard on duty took my arm and led me through the door, I wanted to pull away. It was as if they did everything in their power to make you feel like a prisoner too.

We walked into a narrow room with a row of cubicles. The guard said to Sid, "You can sit here in the corner until it's your turn."

"Luke, do you want me to go first?"

I shook my head. If I didn't do this immediately, I might chicken out. The guard led me to the second cubicle. "Have a seat. Your inmate will be here shortly." My inmate?

I sat down on the hard chair and looked around. It was like a study carrel you might find in a library, except that in front of me stood a Plexiglas window and on the right wall hung a telephone. I wasn't going to see her directly face to face. We were going to have to talk on the telephone. Why hadn't Sid told me? I couldn't convince her this way.

When I looked up, Mom was standing there, swaying back and forth. She shook her head, like she wanted me to go away. She wore this blue outfit, made out of a kind of plastic-looking fabric. The top was stamped with the words "Alameda County." She could have belonged on Alcatraz, except those prisoners had worn stripes and included no females.

She kept shaking her head as she sat down. I stared at her through the scratched and milky glass and felt like I was looking through gauze. She rested both arms on the chair, and leaned toward me. Was she going to refuse to see me? The rules stated that inmates could do that.

Finally she sat down and picked up the phone on her side. I wanted to yell at her to hurry. My twenty minutes were speeding away and with it my nerve.

She began speaking but I couldn't hear her. She tapped on the window and pointed to my telephone. I picked up the old black phone and held the cold instrument to my ear. "I didn't want you to see me here, Luke." Her voice was low and soft. I plugged my other ear to hear her better. "I told Sid not to bring you."

"Mom—"

She tapped on the window again and pointed to her mouthpiece.

I moved my mouth closer. "Mom. I'm here now. Don't send me away. Sid's here, too, waiting by the door. He gets to talk to you next. They almost didn't let me—"

Mom's eyes began clouding over, so I stopped. There was nothing she could do about it. I had more important business and so little time.

"Mom, you did it. You got through the arraignment."

"Thanks for coming to the courthouse, Luke. I didn't expect you." Her voice sounded stronger.

"I'm not sure that I can handle your sentencing."

"I know. But it's the only way I can put this behind me." This was going to be easier than I thought. "They deserve their day in court, too." Her voice broke up over the phone line.

"Wouldn't their forgiveness be better?"

She nodded. "Of course, more than anything in the world."

She gave me an opening.

"So, what if you could meet with the Dolan family and apologize to them privately?"

She leaned close to the glass and I could see her puzzled eyes. "What are you talking about?"

"Mom, they can arrange these face-to-face meetings now

where the person who committed the crime can meet with the victim or the victim's family and—"

She sat there with the phone to her ear, not saying a word. I hated this stupid setup. I couldn't touch her arm or anything. I took a breath and tried to settle down. Now that I'd seen this jail, my idea seemed more important than ever.

"Mom, remember the TV show I watched when the kid talked to the family he robbed and—"

"Luke, I do want to talk to them. But later, when I'm more prepared."

"Thirty-one years hasn't been long enough?" She looked like I had just slapped her. "I'm sorry, Mom." I gripped the telephone. She had to meet with the Dolans when I was around. Maybe it could even lower her sentence when they found out how sorry she was.

"The Dolans will forgive you. Your parents have."

"Have they? I'm not so sure."

Then what was the point of all this, Mom? Of course, they have. They came to see you. They came to the courthouse. They—

"Luke, I've had a lot to deal with." She motioned her hand behind her.

"Didn't you see the paper, Mom?" I heard my voice getting louder. I could be kicked out for yelling. But the guard wasn't looking my way, only Sid.

Before I could stop myself, I said, "You're splattered across the front page of the *San Francisco Chronicle*. It will be worse after that family testifies at your sentencing." She looked like

I'd knocked her over. What an idiot I was. Nobody had showed her the paper. Nobody would.

Why couldn't I be calm, like when I talked to Diane and Sid? Maybe Diane was right. Maybe it was too soon or just a stupid idea and she and Sid were trying to placate me.

I didn't know whether to hang up the phone and leave or not. It was too late for small talk and I'd blown my chance by getting too worked up. I should let her think it over and come back Saturday. But that would be too late. The sentencing was Friday. If she agreed, everything else would work out.

What a laugh. She was in jail. Nothing could change that or the fact that Stephen Dolan was dead.

Mom had put her hands to her eyes, and was wiping away tears. I'd ruined a really good idea by pushing too hard.

"I just thought that this was something that could help and that I could be part of, Mom. Amy's family met with the drunk driver and it really helped them."

"I do want to talk to them, Luke. But this has all taken a lot out of me."

"But when and if you finally meet with the Dolans, I'll miss that, too. I've been left out of everything, Mom."

She looked down at her hands and didn't speak for what seemed like minutes. Finally she looked up. "Maybe you're right, Luke. I certainly owe it to you to give it a chance. But I'm scared. I feel that I need more time. But waiting probably won't make it any easier and if it means this much to you—"

I felt like I was holding my breath. Come on, Mom.

"How would we set it up?" I let out some air.

I explained that Diane would take care of it. She asked me about staying at Amy's, but the guard was already there to get me. I tapped on the glass and waved goodbye. When I tried to stand up, my legs felt like they would buckle. The guard grabbed my arm and this time I didn't mind.

Sid asked me if I wanted to wait there or in the car. What a choice. I wasn't going back to the lobby alone. I tried to close my eyes, hoping the time would pass quickly. I didn't want to see Sid's sagging shoulders or watch him leaning into the glass as if he could touch her.

I tried not to look at my watch either. But finally I couldn't help it. Only ten minutes gone. When I was talking to her, the minutes had flown by. I began hyperventilating. I'd last about a day in jail before going berserk.

Finally Sid stood there with the guard. He took my elbow as we got back on the cart. His arm was shaking.

Chapter 18

Diane seemed pleased that Mom had agreed to a meeting with the Dolans. "Good work, Luke. Your mother sounded very positive about it this morning at the jail. And the prosecuting attorney has already spoken to Mrs. Dolan, and she too is anxious to meet with your mother."

"So then we'll meet Friday morning?" I couldn't believe it had all happened so fast.

"Well, that's the only glitch. Under no circumstances will the judge allow the meeting to take place before the sentencing. The sentencing will be in the morning as planned and the meeting Friday afternoon after lunch."

"No. Mom needs to apologize first, so she doesn't have to speak at the sentencing. The Dolans could say terrible things if they don't know how sorry she is. Mom's been through a lot, especially at that awful jail."

"Luke, your mother is holding up better than you think.

The Dolans want to attend a meeting with her. That indicates they'll be fair in court."

"You can't promise that."

"Luke, you don't have to go to the sentencing."

"So you don't want me to go, Sid?"

"I didn't say that."

"What's the big deal? Why can't we just switch the two meetings around? It's the same day."

"These meetings are never held before the sentencing. Judges don't want them to alter the outcome."

"But the sentence has already been agreed upon." I got up and started pacing.

"Luke, it's not debatable. Diane has other cases besides ours. We need to get going."

"But this is not how I had it planned."

"Since when does life work out like we've planned?"

"How does the old joke go?" Diane asked. "You want a good laugh? Tell God how you've planned your life." Sid thought that was very funny. Both he and Diane smiled and that made me furious.

Then Sid looked at my face. "You weren't even going to come to the arraignment, remember? Now you're running the show." What a joke. I couldn't control anything.

"Do you have any idea how much work it took Diane to set up your mom's plea bargain?" Sid asked. "She didn't do it for money," he explained. "It's all been pro bono because Diane, too, was against the war. She hasn't charged us a penny."

I felt like an idiot. How come Sid hadn't told me that before? "I had no idea. Thank you for helping my mom."

"I was happy to, Luke. You know, the legal world isn't as glamorous as it seems on TV. It involves a lot of writing letters, making phone calls, and waiting and waiting, and then more letters and more phone calls. It all takes a long time. That's why getting this meeting set up so quickly is amazing. I think your being involved helped and the fact that everybody is from out of town. The Dolans live in southern California and need to get home."

I had never thought about where the Dolans might be from.

"Where will it be held?" Sid asked.

"That's good news, too. Sometimes they allow the use of the courtroom if it's available and our judge has agreed."

"That sounds good," Sid said.

"I still wanted the meeting before lunch."

"Generally these meetings are held just between the offender and the victim or the victim's family. I won't be there since it isn't a legal proceeding."

"What about the offender's family?" I asked. "Can't Sid and I be there?"

"There will only be two from the Dolan family, so the facilitator suggested your mother just have one support person," Diane explained.

"But that's not fair. I thought of the idea. I have to be there. Can't both Sid and I go? I promise I'll just sit there and not say a word." They couldn't do this to me. I deserved to sit in on this meeting. My mom wouldn't even be doing it if it weren't for me.

I looked over and Sid was smiling. "Your mother wants you to be her support person, Luke."

"But—"

"I'm glad she chose you. You've earned it."

"But what about you and the rest of her family?"

"Everybody will be fine with it," Sid said.

I sat there wondering how I was supposed to sleep that night.

After Mom's case was called, the judge entered and began the proceedings. "Would anyone like to speak before I pronounce the defendant's sentence?"

The prosecuting attorney rose. "Your Honor, I would like to invite Joan Dolan Ryan, representing the victim's family, to come forward."

A woman about Mom's age slowly walked up to the witness stand and sat down. She was brown-haired and dressed in a black suit with a white blouse. Her face looked eerily like Stephen Dolan's in the old newspaper photograph.

She began reading from a typewritten script, her low, modulated voice polished and devoid of emotion. "Your Honor, it is important for my family that I speak today at the sentencing of the last of the radicals who caused my brother Stephen's death in 1970. Steve was two years older than I. I was a high school cheerleader, enjoying football games and dances, but Steve was the opposite: quiet and peace-loving. He played the French horn, wrote for the school paper, and liked to read. You might even call him an intellectual. I'd heard murmurings of war and seen a few newscasts of American soldiers in a jungle far away, but the Vietnam War hadn't yet affected my life, or maybe I was too busy to pay attention." She stopped and took a drink of water, her voice beginning to waver.

"I was surprised when Steve joined the Army ROTC at Cal. I shouldn't have been. My father was career military and had encouraged my brother to join ROTC as a way of paying for college. My father went to his grave still regretting that. He used to say, 'If only I'd let him take out a loan, Steve would still be with us today.'"

I clenched my fists. This was worse than visiting Mom in jail.

"But that isn't the point. Nor is the question of why he was in that office at one o'clock in the morning. Mary Margaret Cunningham and the others had every right to protest the Vietnam War. But not the way they did it." Her voice rose a notch and she put down the paper.

"No matter how valid the cause, the use of violence is never justified. Endangering life for any reason is never acceptable. And we"—she looked up and out at the courtroom—"have a duty to teach young people today that they are responsible for their actions and that the consequences of those actions can last a lifetime. My family will never recover from the loss of our son and brother." She took another drink of water and picked up the paper.

"Do I hate Mary Margaret Cunningham?" Beside me, Sid's body tensed. Up at the table Mom put her face in her hands. "Not anymore. I know that she did not purposely set out to harm my brother. But I hate what she and her cohorts did. Because of their wrong-sighted and irresponsible actions, my family lost Steve forever.

"Ms. Cunningham's time in jail will not bring my brother back. But now that the last of my brother's perpetrators has come to justice, he may finally be put to rest."

When she sat down, several family members leaned over and hugged her. We all watched, including the judge. After a moment, the judge pounded her gavel. But she didn't need to. Not a sound could be heard. Why did I ever think a meeting could help? This was enough. This was too much.

Finally the judge spoke. "Will the defendant please rise." Mom and Diane stood up. "Ms. Cunningham, do you have anything you wish to say?"

"I do, Your Honor." Her voice sounded clear and strong. Mom walked up to the witness stand. "First of all I apologize with all my heart to the Dolan family. I never would have set a bomb if I'd known someone was inside the gym. I am so sorry, so very, very sorry. Every day since then I have wished I could live that day over.

"I was raised to believe that if something was wrong, you work to change it. Regrettably, when the nonviolent protests against the war didn't seem to be working, I agreed to use more violent means. Ms. Ryan, you are absolutely right. We have all paid the price for my being young and foolish and not considering the consequences. All I can do is ask for your forgiveness and pray that young people today use better judgment than I." Again the room was silent as Mom returned to the table and stood beside Diane. Nobody could doubt her sincerity.

Except the judge. She took a deep breath and stared out at Mom. "It appears that you, Mary Margaret Cunningham, alias Faith McHenry, have led an exemplary life since committing your crime thirty-one years ago. Thankfully you have now finally realized your responsibility to atone for that crime. As judge in this case, I have no choice but to abide by the plea bargain agreement of involuntary manslaughter and a sentence of six years."

She paused and looked around the crowded courtroom. "Let it be noted, however, that I do not consider this sentence severe enough for a crime of this gravity. I too participated in protests against the Vietnam War, Ms. Cunningham. But like thousands of others, I did not resort to violence. As Ms. Ryan so well said, the use of violence to support a cause is never acceptable. Don't you or anyone else in this courtroom ever forget that.

"Furthermore, I will not honor your request"—the judge looked directly at Mom—"to be sequestered in prison in Alaska or Washington state. You will serve your time here in the state of California, at whichever facility prison authorities deem most suitable."

With another pound of the gavel, the courtroom rose and

the judge departed for her chambers. The room erupted in loud whispers as Mom was removed by the guard.

"We're so very sorry for what happened to your son," I heard someone say. I looked up just as my grandmother reached out and touched the arm of a silver-haired woman walking down the aisle. The woman patted Grandmother's hand back.

"Mrs. Dolan," Uncle Mark whispered to me.

Diane hurried us out of the courtroom and into a side room. "What is this business about Mary Margaret serving her time in a California prison?" Grandfather asked.

"Folks," Diane said in a calm voice. "We've just had a very favorable outcome. Mary Margaret received the prearranged sentence. We're lucky the judge didn't try to tinker with the plea bargain. It's been done before, you know."

"But can't we do something to get her location changed?" Sid asked.

Diane shook her head. "I was afraid of this, but I didn't want to say anything until I knew for sure. Since Mary Margaret's plea bargain had already been accepted, the prison location was the only thing the judge could control. And control it she did."

"In Washington state an inmate can petition later for a change," Uncle Mark said.

"Yes, that is a definite possibility down here, too, especially for the last six months of her sentence. Often those final months are spent in a halfway house, and we can petition the court to see if that can take place elsewhere. By then Mary Margaret will have had the chance to show what a model prisoner she is."

"So when can we visit Mary Margaret in her new place? We'd like a tour," Grandfather said. I'll bet he was good in business, pressing all the time.

"Unfortunately it could be up to a month before they even move Mary Margaret to the jail reception center where her security status will be evaluated. She'll probably be sent to Valley State Prison for Women in Chowchilla, where they'll also do some medical and psychological testing as well. All that can take up to sixty days. So it might not be until the holidays that she is transferred to her permanent placement."

"They're going to try and see if Mom's crazy?"

"No, Luke. All the inmates have to go through testing. The lower she scores on her security level, the more perks she can get. Hopefully you can then see her in a regular visiting room and not have to use that awful telephone."

I looked at Sid and he looked as sick as I felt. What a roller coaster ride. How could Mom have ever thought this would make things better?

"Then at least we should be able to attend the meeting this afternoon."

"Mr. Cunningham, I've asked Mr. Rodriguez to meet with you. I'm sure he can explain it far better than I."

My grandmother stood up. "You know, I think we're forgetting to look on the positive side. I thought the young woman's statement was heartfelt, yet quite subdued, and that Mary Margaret handled herself admirably." She stopped and coughed into a handkerchief, then continued. "Diane, how can we thank you for all you've done? Could we take you to lunch?"

"Yes, Diane, you've been terrific," Carol said. Then she went over and hugged her mother. "Mom, it's too late. We're already out to lunch and have been for some time."

Grandmother started laughing and we all joined in. It wasn't that funny. But I laughed until tears rolled down my cheeks.

Chapter 20

hree hours after our laughing siege and lunch we were back in Department 202. I was starting to feel like there was a seat with my name on it.

We gathered around the defendant's table. The whole feeling was different from the morning. No judge, no gavel, no audience. Additional chairs had been brought in so all of us could sit down. Diane introduced Peter Rodriguez, who would facilitate the meeting with the Dolans. After we all introduced ourselves, he began explaining how the meeting would work.

"This is a chance for both parties to speak honestly and freely in a less formal setting and to ask each other questions."

"Excuse me, Mr. Rodriguez."

"Yes?" Mr. Rodriguez looked over at my grandfather.

"I still don't understand why we can't all be present." I could feel my heartbeat speed up.

"I'm glad you brought that up, Mr. Cunningham." Mr. Rodriguez cleared his throat. "I understand your desire to support your daughter at this difficult time. But it's critical that Mary Margaret meet with the Dolans alone. She and I discussed all this yesterday at the jail. Now she knows what to expect. I did the same with the Dolans. You see, the goal of a restorative justice meeting like this is communication and understanding. Mrs. Dolan and her daughter need to feel completely at ease for this to work effectively."

"Young man, I'm curious about this restorative justice business. Can you tell us about it?" Grandmother asked.

Mr. Rodriguez smiled. "It actually started around 1976 with Chuck Colson, one of those charged and sentenced for the Watergate break-in under Nixon. He went on to form the Prison Fellowship to support prisoners and their rehabilitation. But it isn't until recently that more of these meetings have been taking place." Boy, this Nixon keeps popping up.

"Thank you. I had no idea it had started so long ago."

"Mr. Rodriguez, we were deeply affected by that boy's death, too," my grandfather said, his voice softer now.

"No question about that, Mr. Cunningham. But with your whole family here, far outnumbering the two of them, the Dolans will likely feel overpowered. That's why I arranged for you to sit down with Mary Margaret right now before the meeting. I know it's been an emotional week, especially this morning." He stopped and looked around. "It's difficult to converse at the jail. I hope this time together will help."

Mr. Rodriguez nodded at Diane and she opened the courtroom door. Mom came in escorted by a guard. I still shivered every time I saw her in handcuffs. She waited patiently while the guard unlocked them. Afterward she walked over. "Thank you for coming again, everyone." Mom turned to Mr. Rodriguez. "How long do we have before the meeting?"

He looked at his watch, then at the clock on the wall. "It's one o'clock now and the meeting is scheduled for two. To be safe, I'd say you could take about forty-five minutes. I'll be here if you need me."

"I think we'll be fine." He nodded and joined Diane in the back of the courtroom. The guard sat near the door.

She looked at us. "I'm sorry that you can't be at the meeting. But I have to do that alone and I hope you'll understand." I wondered if Grandfather knew I would be there. He hadn't looked at me funny—yet.

"Since we're going to be splitting up soon, I wanted to tell you all how much your support has meant." Mom stopped, her voice wavering. "You have put your lives on hold for me. Thank you."

She walked around the table and stopped by her parents. "There was so much we didn't get to say at dinner the night before the arraignment. You hadn't even met Luke yet." Mom smiled at me.

She put her hands on her parents' shoulders. "I've written you a letter, trying to explain things." She handed her father an envelope. "But I have to say aloud one more time how sorry I am for what I put you through all these years."

"Mary Margaret, when you came home from college for

Christmas vacation that year, you tried to explain about the war protests," my grandmother said, taking her hand. "But we didn't listen."

"Nor I," Carol said.

"How the hell did you end up over in Berkeley, anyway?" Grandfather asked. "You won a scholarship to the University of San Francisco. I thought you wanted to become a doctor, or at least marry one." I didn't know Mom had been so smart.

"I went over to meetings at Berkeley, but our daily protests weren't making a dent in Nixon's White House."

Mom sat down next to Carol and rested her hands on the table, one cupped in the other. "After Kent State, I agreed to help blow up ROTC records as a way to get Nixon to sit up and listen."

"You got taken in by that Rick fellow." Who was this Rick? I wondered.

"Dad, I was a big girl. I have nobody to blame but myself."

"I can't condone what you did, Mary Margaret, nor would I ever have. But we wouldn't have turned our backs on you, either. We would have supported you, no matter what."

"Damn it, Mary Margaret," Carol said. "Couldn't you have at least let us know you were safe all these years?" She put her face in her hands. "Do you have any idea how awful it was, not knowing if you were dead or alive? How Mom and Dad had to put up with their friends ignoring them at church?"

"Those weren't our friends, Carol," my grandmother said.

"Why can't you all let this go? It happened thirty-one years ago," I said, unable to stop myself. Sid shook his head at me.

"You didn't live through those years without her, Luke. You've had your mother all your life," Carol said.

"Well, I don't now."

Carol and I glared at each other.

"You're my sister, Mary Margaret. I've missed you." She put her arm around Mom.

"I didn't contact you because I didn't want to put you in jeopardy, or force you to lie to the FBI. I just kept running and running and after a few years it seemed impossible to turn back the clock." Mom stood up and walked over to me. "And when I got pregnant with Luke I couldn't turn myself in and leave him all alone. He was all the family I had, since I'd given you up years before."

"We could have taken care of him while you served your time," Carol said.

"I was so ashamed about what I'd done and didn't think you could possibly forgive me. I thought I should just disappear from your lives."

"Of course we had forgiven you. We love you, dear. You're our daughter."

"Now, Mom. But then? Could you have understood and forgiven me in the beginning? All the shame I brought on our family?"

"Of course," my grandfather bellowed.

"What about the others?"

"Honey, everybody sends their love," Grandmother said. "You have their letters. It was all so sudden. With Gina pregnant and Tim just starting up his computer business . . ."

"So why now, Sis?" Uncle Mark asked. He hadn't spoken up to this point.

"That's the question Luke kept asking me. I couldn't move beyond my sadness and guilt and it got worse as the years went on. I had to see all of you. I didn't even know if Mom and Dad were still alive.

"And yet I felt paralyzed until—" She took Sid's hand. "I met Sid and I trusted him. He's promised to take care of Luke while I am gone." Sid and Mom looked at each other, until Mom turned away.

She looked over at Mark. "Actually I just wanted to hear one of your bad jokes."

"Oh, you mean the one about the—"

They both started laughing.

"Mary Margaret, it's so good to hear you laughing," my grandmother said. "I didn't think I ever would again. You used to laugh a lot, you know."

"Did I? I just remember working hard, Mom. Always afraid I wasn't good enough."

"We pushed you terribly hard. I know that now. Maybe that's why you cracked—"

"No! *No!*" Mom stood up. "The war was wrong. We just never should have used explosives and I certainly shouldn't have run away."

"Yes, dear." Grandmother patted Mom's hand. "That's all in the past. It's time to move on."

My grandmother dug through her purse. "Look at these wonderful pictures. Here's one of the family at your father's eightieth birthday party last summer."

Mom studied the photos, then passed them over to me. "Luke and I have missed out on so much."

Why didn't Mom show them pictures of all the things we'd done? Because she never let her picture be taken.

"I could have tried to get you off," Uncle Mark said. "I *am* the attorney in the family."

"But I did it, Mark. I'm guilty. That's why I couldn't get beyond it. I need to be punished and Diane understood that."

Mark nodded. "But I would have done anything to help. Carol wasn't the only one who missed you." I looked over at Mark. Please hold it together, fella.

"You put us through hell, Mary Margaret," Carol said, crying again. "But I know your life has been worse." It wasn't that bad, I wanted to say. Come on, Mom. Tell them that.

"I had some wonderful times with Luke." I breathed easier.

Mom looked around at her family. "Can you really forgive me?"

"We did, years ago." Grandmother slowly got up out of her chair, and walked around the table. She put her hands on Mom's shoulders. "I just wish you could have known that and our Lord's forgiveness, too."

"It's God who got me here, Mom. I finally figured out that much."

Peter called out from the back of the room. "Mary Margaret, the Dolans will be here soon."

Mom hugged everybody goodbye until she came to me. "I get to have one support person with me at the meeting. Luke has agreed to join me."

I stared down at the table, afraid to look at my grandfather.

Chapter 21

They barely had time to get out of there. Mom and I both went to the restroom and when I returned the Dolans were already seated at the table. I sat next to Mom with the Dolans across from us and Mr. Rodriguez at one end of the table. That was it, just the five of us. No place to hide.

Mr. Rodriguez explained that the purpose of the meeting was to seek some reconciliation. "Are we in agreement that discussing the incident of thirty-one years ago is why we are here?" he asked. We all nodded.

My heart was thumping so loud I figured everybody could hear it. But nobody looked at me. They were focused on Mr. Rodriguez. "This does not need to be a formal process. You may each speak and ask and answer questions or whatever else will help. Joan, I think you wanted to begin."

She placed a framed picture of her brother on the table.

"Just so we don't forget who we are talking about today." Mom squeezed my hand. This was not a good start.

But I couldn't help staring at the photo. He was such an all-American guy, with short brown hair and smiling teeth. It was all so sad.

"Ms. Cunningham, we have agreed to meet with you today because we didn't feel peace or closure from the trials of your other two accomplices. So here we are once again—my mother and myself. My father died ten years ago."

"Please call me Mary Margaret, if you'd like."

"All right. Mary Margaret, as I said in the courtroom, I believe that you did not purposely set out to harm my brother. But I still can't seem to forgive you." Tears pooled in Joan's eyes. "Why did you have to do it?"

"I would give anything in the world to change what happened that night." Mom stopped and took a breath. "We wanted to end the killing in Vietnam."

"And ended up killing an innocent person in America instead."

"Joan, please," Mrs. Dolan said, touching her daughter's arm. "Mary Margaret, I would like to know more about what happened that night."

"Mother, what they did was wrong. The end doesn't justify the means."

"It certainly doesn't," Mom answered. "And I naively thought somebody in our group had checked out the entire gym right before the bomb was due to go off." She kept twirling her wedding ring from Sid. "I had helped place the bomb near the draft records earlier in the evening. Its timer was set for one A.M."

Joan looked like she was going to interrupt.

Mom held up her hand. "Please, I know I am responsible. Nobody made me do it. And I should have made sure about the other details." I couldn't picture my mom sneaking into a building like a spy. It was still so unreal. But not to the Dolans.

"Or not done it at all," Joan said.

"Or not done it at all," Mom repeated. "We also used far more gunpowder than was necessary to blow up a filing cabinet. We knew so little. Here I was majoring in biology and doing all sorts of labs, but I didn't even take the time to do some simple reading on explosives. I was so caught up in the movement that I—"

"Tell us what happened after the bombing," Mrs. Dolan said.

Mom looked confused, like she couldn't believe Mrs. Dolan wanted to know all this. Mr. Rodriguez motioned her to continue. "We didn't know until the next morning that your son had been killed. When I found out, I wanted to die myself. Rick insisted that we go underground immediately." Mom was shaking, like she was reliving a nightmare.

"But the two of us only lasted a week together. It soon became clear that Rick was more into the danger and excitement of explosives than the cause of ending the war." Mom stopped and sat up straighter.

"I've never seen him since."

I thought Mom wanted to put this behind her. This meeting only seemed to be bringing it all back again. I sat there, wishing I'd never thought of it.

Joan was frowning. She seemed to feel the same way. But not Mrs. Dolan. "Mary Margaret, what was your life like? Thirty-one years as a fugitive is such a long time."

Mom mumbled "Forever," then raised her voice. "I traveled to Alaska in 1976 when one of my underground contacts obtained for me the birth certificate of infant girl Faith McHenry."

She gripped the sides of the table. "You don't want to know all this. I deserved every bad thing that happened to me and more. But I knew that nothing could bring your son back. So I just tried to live the best life I could."

"But you didn't turn yourself in," Joan said.

Silence filled the room. Finally, Mrs. Dolan spoke. "Have you done that? Have you led a good life?"

"I've tried. I kept thinking that if I worked hard enough, the guilt would go away. But it hasn't. By hiding all these years, I avoided one prison and created another. I never saw my family. I deprived my son of knowing his relatives."

Mrs. Dolan looked over at me. "Tell me about your mother."

"Luke is here as a support person today," Peter interjected.

"I'd like to hear from the boy, if he is willing," Mrs. Dolan said.

I sat there, feeling faint. It was hot in the courtroom. It felt like they'd turned off the air conditioning. Mom nudged me.

"Mrs. Dolan." I swallowed and started again. "Mrs. Dolan, you and your daughter know my mother as Mary Margaret Cunningham, but she will always be Faith McHenry to me. She gave a lot to other people. Through the fabric store she owned, she and her partner donated tons of fabric to the women's shelter and set up free quilting classes. She cooked meals at the soup kitchen. But she's not perfect. She's messy at home and late all the time."

I clenched my teeth to keep my jaw from shaking and it took me a while to start speaking again. "I'm sorry about your son. I've been really angry at her ever since she told me about it. And I hated that she had lied to me my whole life about who she really was." I swallowed again. "But I think that if I don't forgive my mom for her mistake, I'll be making one of my own." I looked down. Mom took my hand.

"As much as I grieved for the life of Stephen, I didn't realize until I had Luke how deeply the loss of a child could cut into a parent's soul," Mom said. "I am so very, very sorry."

"Thank you," Mrs. Dolan whispered.

"How did you ever get over it?"

"You never really do. My husband insisted that we go and see where Stephen had died. He was right. It was important we visit Harmon Gym and the offices. And now hearing from you about what happened that night, we have more pieces to the puzzle. Somehow you keep going. Just like you did. One foot in front of the other until eventually the pain is more muffled, not as piercing."

"Have you forgiven me?"

Mrs. Dolan nodded. "Long ago. If I hadn't, I couldn't have gone on. And not forgiving you wasn't going to bring Stephen back."

"Luke talked about mistakes. I made two huge ones, Mrs. Dolan. I didn't come forward for the punishment I deserved and I didn't believe that I could be forgiven."

I sat there wondering if *I* had forgiven my mom. I'd started acting like it after the baseball tournament. But was it real?

"I still don't understand why you didn't turn yourself in earlier if you felt so much guilt," Joan said.

"Fear, shame. I don't know. For a long time I just blocked it all out as if my old life never existed. Then after Luke was born, I couldn't do it. I was all the family he had."

"But what about the boy's father?"

"He was killed by a drunk driver before Luke was born."

"That's unfortunate. He could have cared for Luke while you served your time," Joan said.

"So you've had to learn to forgive, too, Mary Margaret," Mrs. Dolan said.

Mom nodded but didn't say anything. I hadn't ever thought about that.

"Your family has been very supportive this week."

"Yes."

"Some parents would have turned their backs."

"They haven't condoned what I did but they have forgiven me."

"Most parents never stop loving their children." Mrs. Dolan patted Joan's hand.

"Young man." Mrs. Dolan looked over at me. "I understand you suggested this meeting. That's quite impressive—that at your age you are so thoughtful. Thank you."

I nodded. But inside I realized it was for me, too.

"Joan, Mrs. Dolan. I wish there were some way I could make restitution."

"You can't. Stephen is gone. But I do believe you are genuinely sorry. I'll pray for you and this young man and your husband. Will you keep us in your prayers?" Tears were sliding down Mrs. Dolan's face.

Mom was crying now, too. When I looked over, so was Joan.

Finally Mom asked, "When are you leaving for home?"

"Right after this. I have to be back at work in San Diego tomorrow morning."

"Oh, that's such a long drive and it's late already."

Standing up, Joan smiled for the first time. "It's been worth it. Mom's seventy-eight but she's a tough old bird."

Seventy-eight? She looked good. I didn't think I wanted to be still kicking at that age.

Mom held out her hand and Joan took it. "Thank you, Joan. I never dreamed something like this was possible."

"But it's also a huge relief. Would you mind if I wrote you sometimes?"

"I'd like that." Mrs. Dolan opened her arms to Mom. I had shivers again. But this time they had nothing to do with handcuffs.

Chapter 22

Everybody was leaving. Uncle Mark said that if I didn't go to dinner that night they'd think I didn't like them. I felt great and the feeling lasted all through the meal. I invited Amy along as a buffer, but it turned out I didn't need one. Everyone liked her. Who wouldn't? And they didn't even seem to notice her wheelchair.

I thought it might be awkward because they hadn't been invited to the meeting. But Grandfather seemed to have recovered and the rest of them just wanted to know what had happened. It was impossible to put into words the powerful feelings in that room that afternoon.

"It was pretty amazing," was all I could say. "And to be honest I don't know if I could be as forgiving as Mrs. Dolan."

They all nodded. They had gotten my mom back.

Aunt Carol asked where I'd gotten the idea to suggest such a meeting. When they found out, they wanted to hear Amy's story, too.

And then thankfully things lightened up. There were more questions, but just idiotic ones about Alaska. Did people live in igloos? No, not even the Eskimos did, except long ago when they went hunting. Was it winter all year long? No, how did they think I learned to play baseball? Amy—did you ride a dog sled to school? Please.

Finally I wrapped it up by telling them the most stupid question I'd ever been asked by a tourist. "Sonny, can you tell me when they turn on the northern lights?"

"Well, ma'am. I'll have to check that one out with the big guy in the sky." They all laughed. My relatives actually thought I was funny.

Even Sid talked more than usual. He told them about the pipeline and how he had helped build it. I'd never known that.

Later at the park Amy taught me how to do wheelies in her chair. She let me practice while she watched from a bench. I felt almost as good as the night we won the Alaska state championship.

But the next day I had to return to the jail. It was Saturday and visiting sessions were open all day. But you still only got twenty minutes. So everybody—Uncle Mark, Grandma, Grandpa, Aunt Carol, Sid, and me—decided to spread our visits out. Sid and I were scheduled last. He picked me up early so we could talk about our plans.

"I don't want to leave, Luke, but I need to get back and earn some money. Those union jobs go flying out the door in the summer, but things are going to slow down here pretty quick and this trip has been expensive."

"Yeah. It's not like we can visit her every day. Amy's parents said I could stay as long as I wanted to, but I think it's been long enough."

"Okay then. Do we stay five more days to see her on Wednesday or do we leave tomorrow?"

"I guess tomorrow." Was I ready? The last two weeks down here had been so unreal. I hadn't even thought about my life in Fairbanks and now didn't want to.

When we pulled into the jail parking lot, I became instantly depressed. The only remotely decent part of that place was the automated cart that sped down the hallway. When I boarded it, I closed my eyes and tried to pretend that I was in a big airport heading for a European adventure.

Sid went first and I waited in the corner. This time I brought a *Sports Illustrated.*

When Sid came to trade places, I didn't look at him. I would be getting more freedom without Mom at home, but he was losing his wife.

There was something different in Mom's eyes. They weren't as haunted. She picked up her telephone. "Thanks for coming, Luke. I know it's hard."

"I can handle it for a little while. But you have to live here."

"Don't worry about me. Like you said, I've had thirty-one years to get ready."

"Mom, I didn't—"

"Shh—I'm just teasing. We used to be able to do that. Sid told me about your plans. It makes sense. You need to get home. But I will miss you so."

"At least Grandpa and Grandma are staying longer."

She smiled. "Mother said they had a wonderful time with you last night."

"Yeah. It was fun. I'm starting to feel more comfortable around them. I'm not sure what to expect since I've never had any relatives before."

"You've missed out on a lot of things."

"Mom, don't go there." I started tapping my fingers on the counter in front of me. This place gave me the creeps.

"They were quite impressed with Amy."

I nodded. "Amy said she'd visit you if you'd like."

"I would. But it's too long a way for her to come."

"Her mom said that when she gets used to the freeways, she can drive herself."

"Oh, my. She is an amazing girl." Mom stopped and took a breath. "Luke, our time is going quickly and we have some things we need to discuss."

"I know. Like adoption. Sid and I will take care of it."

Mom put her hand on her heart. "Luke, I feel like a new person after yesterday's meeting. Thank you for pushing me to do it."

"Yeah. It worked out."

"Much more than that. I slept better last night than I have in—"

"In thirty-one years."

She laughed.

"I guess you were right about what you needed to do."

"Not about everything. It wasn't right not to talk about your father."

"Mom. Sid and I were thinking about coming down for Christmas. You tell me then."

"But I thought you always wanted to know more about him."

"Not now."

"I was so afraid that his family might want to be part of your life and if they found out what I'd done . . ."

I gripped the phone receiver. "Enough of the heavy stuff. I'm fine with it."

"He was a good man, Luke."

I nodded but wanted to get the hell out of there.

"It's long overdue that I told you what he was like."

"Write me a letter." I didn't want this now. Why couldn't she see that?

"His name was Michael Peterson," Mom said softly into the receiver. "He worked as an engineer for British Petroleum at the Prudhoe Bay camp. It's time I finally contact his family and let them know that they have a grandson."

I held up my hand. "No, I've had enough surprises."

She nodded.

"Do I look like him?" I blurted out, before I could stop myself.

"Not really. He was blond, a Norwegian from Minnesota. You are each handsome in different ways." She smiled and tapped the window.

The guard walked up behind my chair. "I hope the high school girls feel the same way. Bye, Mom."

"Take care, honey."

I hung up the phone and stood up. I waved, then turned and walked toward Sid.

Chapter 23

Sid and I returned to Alaska on the thirteenth day of my trip. Amy drove us to the airport. I leaned over to hug her and bumped her cheek instead. I'd have to work on that move.

When she sat, driving the van, it seemed like she was a regular person, that she could walk and run and dance.

Sid and I both insisted that she not come in. I stood on the sidewalk and watched her pull away, waving long after the van had disappeared.

When I got off the plane in Fairbanks I was prepared for reporters or strange looks from people, but nobody except Kathleen and Charlie even noticed us.

A few days later when I finally unpacked my backpack I found my paint grenade in the side pocket. I hadn't thought of it the whole trip. It was like the minute Mom's situation started unfolding in California, I morphed into an adult.

I pulled the grenade out and squished the black plastic, so the paint squiggled around into a different shape. Things could change so fast. I tossed it back and forth between my hands and remembered how excited I'd been the night I found it.

Somehow it had survived the plane trip to California and back and never blown up. Too bad Mom hadn't used one of these instead of a pipe bomb. I wound up my arm like I was going to pitch it. Just one mistake. That's all it took to completely change somebody's life. Can you fix a mistake or just cover it up?

I took a step to throw, then stopped. If Mom hadn't planted that bomb, she'd probably have transferred to Berkeley, graduated with honors, gone to medical school, lived in some fancy house, and flown home to Spokane every Christmas. I wouldn't exist. Stephen Dolan wouldn't be dead.

I heard pounding on the front door but ignored it. After a couple of minutes, Dan came bounding up the deck stairs, yelling my name.

I was glad to see him. But we didn't know what to say, and he didn't tell any of his usual stupid jokes. Surely he'd learned a few in California. Finally he asked about Amy.

"She's okay. She drove me around a lot in her van. That was cool."

"Ever thought about how you would kiss somebody in a wheelchair?"

"Geez, Dan, we're just friends." Amy was like a big sister now and I'd almost forgotten how hot I used to think she was.

"Yeah, right, fella."

"I do wonder how you would do it, though," I finally admitted. "She's so good-looking that somebody's going to fall hard for her eventually and figure it out somehow. I just hope they aren't put off by her wheelchair. It is weird at first."

"Do you think you would have even talked to her if she hadn't worked at your mom's store?"

I shrugged my shoulders and tossed the grenade over to him. I'd like to have said yes, but I wondered if I could have seen her and not just her wheelchair.

"Where did you get this? It's awesome."

"I found it the first time I went paintballing with Lemming." Dan frowned. "You know, he didn't turn out to be so bad on All Stars."

"No, he played well. Kept us in the hunt a couple of times."

"He's still a jerk. But he's what you'd call a tolerable jerk."

Dan looked at me funny. He wasn't going to be convinced about Lemming. "All Stars was great, except when I ended our whole season striking out and—"

"Zip it, McHenry." He began tossing the grenade back and forth in his hands. "Everybody had glimmers of brilliance and moments of madness."

I raised my eyebrows. "My. Did we become a philosopher in Santa Cruz?" He laughed.

"Nah, a beach bum. I bodysurfed in the ocean. I'm thinking about trying a real surfboard sometime. Those surfers are out catching waves night and day."

Dan put the grenade down. "I'm sorry about your mom. When my cousin showed me the newspaper and asked if I knew her, I couldn't believe it. It was like that's my best friend's mother. I'm over at their house all the time." He started picking at the paint on the railing. "And then I understood why you were staying with Amy. I had thought it was kinda weird when you first told me."

"Why? Girls and guys can't be friends?"

"Come on. It's not like you have a bunch of girls as friends."

"Well, I got to know Michelle on the team and we're friends."

"Yeah." Dan nodded. "Michelle turned out all right. She really hung in there. You know, when I heard about your mom, I really wanted to call you, but I didn't have Amy's number or know where she lived. I did call Kathleen at the store and she said you were doing okay and not to worry. Are you okay?"

I started peeling paint with him. "I guess so. If you can call seeing your mom arrested, put in jail, meeting relatives you never knew you had . . ."

"Man. I can't even imagine that."

"I know. If somebody had told me this story, I would have said that it sounded like a bad movie plot."

"So how long had you known about your mom?"

"Only a week or so before All Star tryouts." I looked over at him. "Did I act different?"

He shook his head. I guess I was as good an actor as my mom. Scary. "I figured you didn't know until after we got eliminated from the tournament in California."

"I wanted to tell but I couldn't. Besides, how do you explain to somebody that your mom is wanted by the FBI."

We leaned out over the railing and looked down at Mom's garden. "I can't picture your mom in jail. She was always so nice and quiet."

I didn't want to tell him about the jail. "So what do you think of her now?"

"That something crazy must have happened to her in college."

"It's called Vietnam," I said, kicking the railing. "Do you remember in third grade when we used to write those gory stories in writers workshop?" Dan nodded. "Well, I must have written a lot of them because Ms. Carsons got worried and suggested that I be tested by the school psychologist."

"What? They thought you were going to grow up to be a psychopath or something?" He whistled. "You never told me that."

"I was too embarrassed. That night after the teacher called, I heard my mom talking on the phone to Kathleen, wondering what she'd done wrong as a parent."

Just the other day I'd remembered that story and how scared I'd been before they tested me. I really thought they might discover that I was a violent kid inside, even though I didn't feel like one. I just liked blood and gore.

"So what happened?"

"Oh, I passed with flying colors. The psychologist wrote in her report that I was a kind and loving boy. Funny thing. I wrote about violent things but my mom went out and did them."

"She made a mistake."

"A big one. But her family and even the mother of the kid that died have forgiven her. It's almost unbelievable. The thing is—" I grabbed the grenade off the deck chair. "Oh, I don't know."

What I wanted to say was that everybody makes mistakes and that I probably would, too. But that I didn't want to make one that lasted thirty-one years. I couldn't seem to say it out loud.

"I'll be right back." Dan went inside. He came back holding our phone book. "Hey, let's get ready for freshman English. I read about this kid who writes poetry inspired by the Yellow Pages. I guess you just read the paired headings on every page and go from there."

He handed me the book and I started reading. "Bed-Beer. Bingo-Blowers. Cellular-Cemeteries. Clutches-Cocktail." My mind was blank.

"It has definite possibilities," Dan said, grabbing the phone book from me. "Nothing clicking for you, Lukey

Boy? Let's see. Weed-Welcome. Okay, here's my poem. My dear friend Luke has a yard called Weed Welcome."

"Give me that back. Sheet-Shock. Dan the Man's room gets sheet shock once a year. He throws them in the washer and they quake from all the suds." We started laughing.

"That is bad, really bad. And it doesn't even rhyme."

"Well, you couldn't even finish yours."

"Freshman football starts tomorrow. Let's go out for it."

I hit Dan's arm. "Maybe."

"It's hard to believe we're starting high school next week. Remember how somebody planted that fake bomb the day before school got out?" Did I ever. "Do you think they caught the kids who did it?" Dan looked at me. "Sorry. I guess I shouldn't talk about bombs."

"Man, if you're acting like this, what is everybody else going to do? They're going to treat me like a weirdo because of my mom."

"Nah. It's already yesterday's news."

"Let's get rid of this." I handed the grenade to Dan. "You're the pitcher, let it rip."

"Nope. The honor's all yours."

I wound up and threw it over the fence and into the woods. It splattered against a tree, the orange paint dripping down the trunk and into the leaves for several feet in every direction. The stain could last a while.

Chapter 24

Usually by mid-August it would be raining and the nights cool—sure signs of winter ahead. But this year it stayed hot, and every day another warm weather record was broken, as if Sid and I had brought the California climate back with us. I wish Mom could have been here for it. Her flowers were still blooming like crazy.

She'd already written us a letter with complete instructions.

> Cut down the perennials and cover them with leaves. That way they'll come back strong next May. I wish I had enjoyed this time of year more, instead of always worrying that the cold and dark days were on their way.

My grandmother sent me some photos of when Mom was a kid. I could be imagining things, but in one photo I actually looked like her. Sid agreed.

Lemming invited me to his birthday party and a bunch of us played paintball in the empty lot near his house. At first I couldn't get into it, until I remembered how much fun we'd had the night we played as a team against the military guys.

After football practice one day I biked home past the church. The priest was outside pulling weeds. He waved and I pulled over. I thought he'd ask about my mom, but he just wanted to know how I was doing and we started talking. Out of the blue I asked, "So how come some people die young and others die old?"

"Maybe some of us just have more to learn."

One night Mom called collect. She told us about tutoring in the learning center and finally losing weight because the food was so bad. "I miss you guys. Luke, are you still on?"

"Yeah, Mom."

"I remembered something the other day. In the bottom drawer of my dresser under my winter sweaters is a photograph of your father when he was a child. I thought you'd like to have it."

I found the photograph. He was about six years old, standing there grinning and wearing a baseball cap. I got out Mom's photo and laid them side by side on my dresser.

Kathleen asked me one night if I was going to change my name. But to what? I could make up a new name, like Luke McKeeham, or follow the rule for great sports names that Lemming had given us in California—a two-syllable first name and three-syllable last name, like Lucas McHenry.

Luke Cunningham. Luke Peterson. Those names were part of me. But I'd been Luke McHenry all my life. Why should I change it now? Names don't matter—or do they?

Were Faith McHenry and Mary Margaret Cunningham the same person but just with two names? I asked Uncle Mark about that. He said that she seemed mostly the same, that she had always stood up for things. Always been a little naive, too.

Honk. Honk. Honk. The long, piercing sounds of sandhill cranes drove me out onto the deck. Overhead, the birds flew in a V formation, finally heading south for winter. Summer was officially over. School started tomorrow.

It seemed like only yesterday the birds had arrived at Creamer's Field, resting on their way to the Arctic. I shook my head. No, it was April, a lifetime ago before All Stars, before Amy, before I knew about Mary Margaret Cunningham, Stephen Dolan, or Michael Peterson.

One leader, eight following close behind. Dark wings stretched out, green-crowned heads held high. I watched, waiting for the leaders to switch. Finally, they did.

Once when I was little, Mom had told me, "That's how they survive. They take turns flying into the wind, Luke."

Now it's my turn. But I'm not alone. Mom wasn't either, she just couldn't believe it. I'm going to hang onto Luke McHenry, at least for now. Mom gave me that name and it will always be mine.